ANOTHER ME

By the same author

Run, Zan, Run
Missing
Bad Company
Dark Waters
Fighting Back

ANOTHER ME

CATHERINE MACPHAIL

BLOOMSBURY

First published in Great Britain in 2003 by Bloomsbury Publishing Plc
38 Soho Square, London, W1D 3HB

A CIP catalogue record of this book is available from the British Library

ISBN 0 7475 6460 4

Printed in Great Britain by Clays Ltd, St Ives plc

3 5 7 9 10 8 6 4 2

To Kathryn
who suggested I write a ghost story

CHAPTER ONE

'Here comes Fay Delussey, always got her nose in a book!'

I jumped when I heard my name, and bumped into my friends, Kaylie and Dawn, as they ran up to me. Dawn snatched the book from my hands.

'What are you reading anyway? Must be good.' Her face crumpled when she read the title on the spine. '*All Quiet on the Western Front.*' She giggled. 'Sounds *so* interesting . . . NOT!'

As you can tell Dawn wasn't much of a reader and she thought she was funny.

'It's about the First World War,' I told her. 'I'm trying to get it finished before I hand it back to the library. Don't want to have to pay a fine for it being late.'

Kaylie sighed. 'Reading about a war. Honestly, Fay. Why don't you read something good for a change . . .'

Her voice became a whisper. 'Like Stephen King.'

'Don't like ghost stories,' I reminded her, 'or anything scary.'

Dawn rolled her eyes. 'We know ghost stories don't happen in real life, Fay. That's why we enjoy them. Whereas war—' She pushed my book back at me as if it was contaminated. 'Now that's real, and that *is* scary.'

I knew she was right, of course. Ghosts aren't real. Ghost stories don't happen. Not in real life. But they scare me anyway.

'Better hurry if you're going to the library.' Kaylie gave me a push. 'Or you'll be late for drama.'

'Does Daft Donald still want us to put on a play?' I groaned at the thought of it. Donald Moffat was one of our English teachers and was always trying to get our class interested in play acting. That's what made him so daft.

Kaylie and Dawn groaned too. 'Shakespeare.' They said it through gritted teeth.

'Shakespeare?' I couldn't believe it. 'Is he off his chump?' We all pretended to be sick in the corridor. 'I hate Shakespeare. People talking funny and being mistaken for other people. Who'd ever believe that?'

'At least we'll get to dress up,' Dawn said.

'Unless he decides we've to play it in the nude.'

Kaylie shrieked at the thought of that and sent Dawn and I into another fit of the giggles.

'Hope it's *Romeo and Juliet*,' Kaylie said. Her eyes moved beyond my shoulder. 'And here comes Romeo.'

I turned to look, though I knew exactly who she was talking about. Drew Fraser. Most of the girls in our year fancied him. Though not half as much as Drew fancied himself. I was not one of his admirers. I knew him too well. Always had done. He lived on the second floor of our high block of flats. Eleven floors below me, and beneath me in every way.

I had grown up with Drew, been to every one of his birthday parties and he was always invited to mine. Our mums were friends from way back. I've found it's very difficult to fancy someone when he's bashed you with a fire engine (his third birthday), tried to stuff a chicken on your head (his fifth), and sunk his teeth into your arm and drawn blood (his sixth, if I remember correctly).

He's still a bit of a vampire even now. He loves reading about the occult, and any kind of psychic phenomena. He's a weirdo if you ask me. If my friends could see his room, hung with skeletons and masks and monsters, they would think he was a weirdo too. Of course, seeing his room counted as a lifetime ambition for Kaylie and Dawn.

However, it seemed mine was the minority view. Drew Fraser had grown from a knock-kneed boy into a weirdo who was tall and handsome. He was long and thin, with floppy dark hair and a lopsided grin. His green eyes sent most of the girls into orbit. He flashed them now in our direction.

'Hello, girls.' He threw the words at us as if he had scattered precious jewels among his harem. Then he swaggered past us. Dawn watched him with her mouth hanging open.

'He is gorgeous, by the way,' she said.

I hurried off and left them both mooning after him.

Actually, hurried is the wrong word. I was too busy reading to hurry. Too anxious to finish my book to even look where I was going. So I didn't notice the someone I brushed against as I went into the library. I muttered an apology and was vaguely aware of a green sweater, just like mine, going out as I went in.

Yet, in that second, something ice cold shivered down my spine, as if someone had just walked over my grave. That's what they say, isn't it? Someone walking over your grave?

At the desk, Mrs Watt, the school librarian, was busy pinning up another poster. I had to tap the desk to make her turn round and notice me.

'Hello, Fay. Did you forget something?'

She must have noticed my puzzled frown. 'I've only just come in,' I said.

'Didn't you just leave?' Her eyes moved to the door.

I shook my head. 'I came to return this book.'

Her eyes were still on the door leading out of the library. 'My goodness, I could have sworn that was you.' She brushed the notion away with a toss of her head. 'Oh well, they do say everyone has a double somewhere.'

It was only as I was walking to the drama class that I remembered the girl I had bumped into and the green sweater just like mine. That was what had got Mrs Watt mixed up. She had seen the girl in the green sweater and thought it was me.

That was the simple explanation.

Wasn't it?

CHAPTER TWO

The school auditorium was buzzing. It seemed most of our year had stayed behind for the auditions. I spotted Kaylie and Dawn in the corner and waved.

As soon as I was close enough they enveloped me in their arms, as if they hadn't seen me for years.

'Po-faced Monica thinks she's going to get the lead part,' Dawn whispered in my ear. My eyes shot across the room to where Monica Meldrum stood, holding court with her groupies. She tossed back her thick blonde hair and pouted. Monica wasn't in our set . . . or rather we weren't in hers. We weren't clever enough, or good looking enough. Of course, the main reason was that we didn't hang on her every word.

She glanced over and caught me looking at her. 'You got a problem, Delussey?' she sneered. She'd never do that if she could see herself. That sneer turned her pretty face into something hideous.

'Yeah, I've got to look at you.' That's what I wanted to say, but I could never be bold enough to do that. Instead, I blushed. No matter how hard I tried I couldn't stop myself.

'Oh look, she's going red,' one of Monica's lapdogs piped up. 'She's just so chuffed you actually spoke to her, Monica.'

Just then Daft Donald, the drama teacher, stepped up on to the stage. He clapped his hands to get us all to shut up. 'I'm delighted so many of you stayed for the auditions.' He beamed a smile around the room. 'All the other teachers said I was crazy to attempt Shakespeare, and I told them you would love to do it. And I was right, eh?'

That's why we called him daft. He hadn't figured out the real reason was that if we were in his play we would be excused other classes. He rubbed his hands together enthusiastically. 'So are we all ready to give Shakespeare a bash?'

'Somebody should have bashed him long ago,' a voice shouted from the back and we all laughed. All, except Donald.

'I am going to help you appreciate the beauty of

13

Shakespeare's language – his passion for words.'

'BORING!' the same voice called, and the groan that went throughout the auditorium showed we were all in agreement.

Donald ignored it. 'We are going to do *The Tragedy of Macbeth*. Or . . . the "Scottish Play", as they call it in the theatre.'

Another communal groan.

'There's hardly any parts for girls in that, sir,' an aspiring starlet at the front reminded him.

'I realise that,' Donald said, nodding his head like a toy dog in the back seat of a car. 'So some of the girls will be taking men's roles.'

That nearly caused a riot.

'Told you,' I muttered to Dawn, 'it's going to be *so* unbelievable.'

'Can we not do a different play, sir?' one of the boys suggested. 'What about *Reservoir Dogs*?'

Donald knew he was losing what little enthusiasm we had. 'You want blood and guts, boys. Well, there's plenty of that in the "Scottish Play". It's wonderful. There's fighting.' He looked around the boys hopefully.'There's passionate love and murder.' His eyes turned on the girls. 'There's even a ghost.'

'I hate ghosts,' I whispered.

'And there's witchcraft. What more could you ask for?' Everyone still looked bored. Daft Donald let out a long sigh. His voice changed. 'We're doing *Macbeth* whether you like it or not.'

By this time hardly anyone was interested in his daft old play. When he clapped his hands for our attention, it took ages for anyone to listen.

'We're going to put on the play during Christmas week, for the entertainment of the whole school.'

I nudged my friends. 'The whole school will be delighted, I'm sure.'

Donald carried on. 'I'll read out to whom I've allocated the main parts, and we'll start rehearsals on Tuesday.'

There was a murmur of protest. 'Sir, what about the auditions?'

Daft Donald sometimes wasn't as soft as he looked. 'I teach you, remember? I know what you're all capable of. I have decided who is playing the parts. OK?'

'That's not fair, sir.'

Donald gave a superior little smile. 'This is not a democracy.'

I turned to my friends. 'Well, I'm definitely not playing a man.'

15

'I wanted to dress up in a fancy frock,' Dawn moaned.

'Maybe we could be the three witches,' said Kaylie and we all giggled.

'Macbeth is going to be played by Andrew Fraser.'

A sigh fluttered around the room, but no one was very surprised. Drew Fraser was always favourite to land the main part. No wonder half the boys hated him.

'And, after careful consideration, the part of Lady Macbeth . . .' There was an ever so slight hesitation. I glanced across at Monica, already preening herself for stardom. '. . . goes to Fay Delussey.'

To say I was gobsmacked just isn't strong enough. I hadn't heard him properly, surely. Me? The main part?

Dawn and Kaylie were jumping about and hugging me, but I couldn't say a word. Monica's face had gone red as a beetroot as she tried to look as if she didn't care a bit, and failed.

'But why me?' I whispered to my friends. 'I don't understand.'

Dawn thought she had the answer. 'Sometimes, when I catch you looking out the window in class, there's something about you. Strange. As if you were in another world. As if you weren't quite right in the head . . . exactly like Lady Macbeth. She goes mad, doesn't she?'

I wasn't sure for a moment if she was joking or serious. 'Are you trying to be offensive? As if I "weren't quite right in the head"?' And she was supposed to be my friend. 'Thank you very much,' I said, but I was laughing. 'Mad indeed!'

'No, I didn't mean totally mad . . . I meant, just kinda daft looking.'

'You're digging yourself in deeper and deeper, Dawn!' Kaylie said, clamping her hand across Dawn's mouth. Now we were all giggling again.

The other parts were finally allocated, and Dawn and Kaylie were to be two of the three witches. But, as for Monica, there was not a mention. And was she mad! When Donald was finished she couldn't keep quiet any longer. 'And what about me, sir, am I not going to be in this play at all?'

Donald grinned at her. 'Of course you are, Monica. I want you to be Fay's understudy.'

I was sure I saw Monica's blonde hair stand on end. My understudy! She would go bananas about that. Monica glared over at me. I tried to smile back at her, but it just wouldn't come. The look on her face was just too scary.

'Me! An *u-u-understudy*!' She stuttered out the words.

Donald was nodding again. 'Yes. There is a resemblance between you two girls, same colouring, same height. So I don't want you in the play together. People could get mixed up. Especially people in this school, who are a bit thick anyway. You'll be a wonderful understudy, Monica. You'll get the lead in the next play, I promise.'

Monica sucked in her cheeks and looked as if she was about to explode.

We all left for home after that. My friends and I bustled out of the school, still laughing at the thought of poor old Monica being only an understudy.

An icy mist had descended on the November afternoon and the smirr of rain seemed to seep deep into the bones.

Suddenly, a furious Monica rushed up behind me.

'Don't look so smug, Delussey!' She pulled me round to face her. 'You know how you got that part, don't you?'

'Talent?' I teased, pleased I had actually had the nerve to say it and not just think it.

18

'Talent, nothing!' she snapped. 'Daft Donald feels sorry for you. Everybody knows about your mum and her boyfriend. Your mum and dad'll be splitting up soon. That's how you got the part!'

I was so angry I wanted to lash out and slap her. I wanted to cry, but I wouldn't, not in front of her. Monica looked so smug. Dawn and Kaylie pulled me away from her.

'Don't bother with her, Fay. She's not worth the trouble.'

Monica just couldn't let it go. 'I'll get you for this, Delussey,' she called after me. 'I'm going to make you really sorry.' There was a viciousness on her face that was really frightening. 'I'll get that part, you see if I don't. One way or another.'

CHAPTER THREE

As Dawn and Kaylie walked with me to the top of the long stairs that led down to my tower block, they kept trying to make me feel better about what Monica had said.

'Don't listen to her, Fay. She's so full of hot air.'

'But why *did* Donald give me the part?' I kept asking them, knowing they couldn't know the answer either. I hadn't shone in any of his past productions, hadn't had any part even near the lead. So why choose me to play Lady Macbeth? Did he just feel sorry for me?

Neither Kaylie nor Dawn knew what to say. The story had been a bit of a scandal at the school not long ago. It seemed everyone had known long before Dad or I that my mother had a boyfriend. I'd seen her with him once, the man she worked with, sitting in a car and I hadn't even realised there was anything suspicious about it. She was my mum after all. Mums didn't have boyfriends. Not mums like mine.

But she had. And when she'd finally confessed to Dad there had been arguments and discussions and for a while, a terrifying while, I was sure she was going to leave. But she didn't. Instead, she had given him up. She had even changed her job. The arguments had stopped, but in their place an atmosphere as cold as the grave had settled on our flat. Dad didn't trust her any more, and Mum never looked happy.

No wonder I was always lost in a book. With my nose in a book I could forget for a while what was happening at home.

When we reached the top of the stairs I said decisively, 'I'm going to tell him tomorrow he can stuff his part. I don't want anyone feeling sorry for me.'

Kaylie was shocked. 'Don't be stupid. You can't let Mucky Monica get that part. Especially not after what she said today.'

Dawn agreed. 'No way, Fay. Just think of the fun we're going to have watching her face every day, having to be *your* understudy.'

In the end, very reluctantly, I agreed. To make Monica suffer like that had to be worth something.

As I left them and began the trek down the stairs the mist thickened into a fog, swirling round the dim lights that hung over the walls on either side of the stairs. Dad didn't like me coming home this way. The stairs were long and narrow, with high walls on either side, with only the odd light dimly illuminating the path. Trees hung over the wall too, and even on a bright summer day the stairs were dark and dismal. But on a night like this, with the fog drifting in and out of the branches, they were worse than dismal. They were eerie. But it was a shortcut everyone used. If I didn't come down these stairs the route home through streets and avenues would take at least another fifteen minutes.

It was always busy.

Except for today.

Funny, I thought, that there was no one on the stairs today. It was true that most of the school had left earlier, but I had never known it to be *so* deserted.

The fog, I supposed. More people taking the bus home, or finding the idea of the stairs too eerie in the dark afternoon.

Even sounds were muffled in the fog. Hoots from cars, a distant fog horn sounding on the river, all had a strange weird sound.

I was halfway down when I heard them.

Footsteps clipping behind me. Someone coming down the steps at exactly my speed. I stopped for a second and the clipping stopped too. It made me smile. It was an echo, I realised. A muffled echo of my own steps.

And yet—

When I began to walk again, there they came behind me, clip, clip, clip. I had never before heard my feet echo on these steps.

I began to hurry. The feet behind me speeded up as I did. Surely, it had to be an echo. Still, the sound was making my heart beat faster. It was as if they were after me – coming down behind me, the footsteps and whoever they belonged to, shrouded by the fog.

I stopped again, abruptly, and so did they. But surely, this time, they stopped a moment after me?

But, not an echo.

Someone else.

Someone else, hidden in the fog.

'Who's there?' I called out.

There was no answer. Still, I was sure there *was* someone, out of my sight, standing waiting in the fog behind me.

Who? What?

Without realising it I was pressing myself against the wall, holding my breath. I was afraid, and I wondered what I was afraid of.

What was the most frightening thing that could come out of that fog?

CHAPTER FOUR

I didn't have time to think about that. There was a sudden rush and something, someone, came lunging at me.

I let out a shriek and almost fell.

It was Drew Fraser.

It had been him all along.

'Look who it is, Lady Macbeth. I've always wanted to be married to a wimp.' He made a face at me. They wouldn't think he was so good looking if they could see him now, I thought.

'Don't you dare call me a wimp!' But my voice was soft, not harsh the way I wanted it to be.

'Well, let's face it. You as Lady Macbeth isn't exactly typecasting, is it?'

'I suppose you would have preferred Monica.'

He shrugged his answer. An answer that seemed to say anyone would be better than me.

'Was that you up there, trying to frighten me?'

He rolled his eyes. 'I wouldn't have to do much to frighten you, would I?'

I wouldn't let him see he'd managed it.

If I'd had the nerve I would have asked him if he would walk down the stairs with me, but then he would definitely think I was a wimp. I just didn't want to walk home alone through this fog. Not today.

But Drew paused only for a moment. 'See you at rehearsals!' He laughed, and gave my bag a punch that lifted it from my arms and sent books and jotters flying all over the ground.

'Oops, sorry,' he laughed. Then he was gone, taking the stairs two at a time, swallowed up by the fog.

'Hate you, Drew Fraser,' I shouted after him. I bent down and began to pick up my books. 'I'll show him who can act!' I muttered to myself.

He had only made me more determined that I would take the part. I'd show him, and Monica, and even Daft Donald, that Fay Delussey was no wimp. I wasn't some-one you could feel sorry for. In a way, I thought, I was glad I had bumped into Drew. Nothing was going to stop me playing Lady Macbeth now.

I began again to clip down the stairs, and even my

steps seemed to echo my determination. They sounded sure of themselves, just like me at that moment. Not like Drew Fraser's soft tread as he'd run away from me.

I stopped dead.

Drew Fraser's soft tread.

Those footsteps behind me. Those clipping footsteps so like my own. They couldn't have belonged to Drew.

Because, I suddenly realised, Drew Fraser had been wearing trainers.

CHAPTER FIVE

Mum wasn't home. Only Dad, sitting by the heater pretending to read his paper. But I could see him all the time glancing at the clock as it ticked the minutes away.

'Fog's awful,' I said, and he grunted. 'That's probably why Mum's late.'

He stared at me over his glasses and didn't say anything for a minute. Then he smiled and put down his paper. 'You're probably right, honey. Now, how about you? Did you have a good day?'

He got up and followed me into the kitchen while I told him about getting the part.

'*Macbeth!*' He whistled. 'Your teacher's being a bit ambitious. That's a hard play even for adults.'

'Oh, he's adapted it for us, to make it easier, he says.'

'So, who's Macbeth?' But he answered the question himself. 'Not Drew the heart-throb? He seems to get picked for everything these days. Football, drama. You name it and he's the star.'

I tutted. 'He's bribing someone if you ask me. I certainly don't think he's a heart-throb.'

'That's because you've known him so long. You can remember him growing up. Skin and bone, with legs like sticks. If ever there was a case of an ugly duckling turning into a swan, it's Drew Fraser.' We both laughed at the memories. Drew Fraser's mum and mine had been friends for a long time. Now, his mum drove mine potty with her tales of her wonderfully talented son. She had forgotten the years when Drew couldn't walk in a straight line without tripping over his shoelaces.

Dad shook his head. 'So he's landed the star part.' He started to peel potatoes. 'You know, *Macbeth* is supposed to be an unlucky play. In the theatre they won't even call it by its real name.'

'Donald told us. The "Scottish Play", they call it.'

'Yes, it has a history of weird things happening when it's on.'

I remembered then the weird thing that had happened to me on the stairs, in the fog, and that strange feeling I had that someone was there watching me, following me. I was just about to tell Dad, when we heard

29

Mum's key in the lock and my dad stiffened. He dropped a half-peeled potato into the sink and headed for the door. I was forgotten.

'Couldn't get a bus!' Mum shouted. 'The fog's so thick some of the buses have been taken off so I had to walk.'

'That's what we thought,' I said quickly and ran past Dad into the hall to kiss her. 'Didn't we, Dad?'

He didn't answer. He just looked at her, as if he wasn't sure she was telling the truth. There it was again, that icy atmosphere. They would spend the rest of the night talking to each other without really saying anything, and never meeting each other's eyes.

I told her about the part and she made all the right noises.

'My daughter the star! Wait till I tell Drew's mum that! At least it's not just her wonderful son who can get star billing!'

But she wasn't really listening. Just as Dad hadn't really listened. And later as I lay in bed I could hear them arguing softly in the living room. He still didn't trust her. She still wasn't happy.

I cried myself to sleep. I so much wanted them to stay together. They were the two most wonderful people in the whole world. Why couldn't they be happy? If they split up, I didn't know what I'd do. I'd be torn between them. I loved them both.

Next morning, they had both gone off to work by the time I left the flat for school. I met old Mrs Brennan at the lift. She was our next-door neighbour. Nosy, but nice. She knew everything about everybody, but she was always doing people favours, always knitting for some-one, or baking for them.

'That you off to school, honey?' she said.

Stupid question. I was in my uniform, hardly likely to be going to a pop concert. 'Yes, Mrs Brennan,' I said.

'My you've got bonny hair,' she said, flicking my shiny bob with her hand. 'It's always that bouncy look-ing. Healthy. In this day and age you don't often see healthy hair like that.'

'This day and age' was Mrs Brennan's favourite expression. She used it all the time.

The lift arrived and as the doors creaked open I let Mrs Brennan step inside.

'Look at the state of me,' she said, pointing to her reflection in the mirrored steel at the back of the lift. 'You'd never think I used to have hair as bonny as yours.'

31

I compared the two of us. Mrs Brennan with her tight curls like a steel scouring pad. And me, with my hair bouncy and shiny and blonde. The mirror made the lift look bigger. I was glad of that. It took away from the feeling that when the doors slid closed you might have been locked in a steel coffin.

We were past the ninth floor when it began to shudder.

'Not again!' Mrs Brennan moaned, and we watched as the lights above the doors tracked our progress to the ground. 9-7-5-. Suddenly, with one almighty shudder it came to an abrupt halt.

'It's always this odd lift that breaks down.'

She didn't notice my smile. Only my reflection saw that, and it smiled too. I winked at myself. The odd lift. Such a funny expression, summing up perfectly the contraption that served the odd-numbered floors in our tower block. The lift *was* odd, and strange and weird. Breaking down, refusing to open doors, or close them. Shuddering and shaking. Always causing problems. Always trapping someone inside. As if it had a life of its own.

'They never have a problem with the even lift,' Mrs Brennan went on. 'See this lift … it's going to kill somebody one of these days.'

32

Cheery thought, Mrs Brennan, and I winked at my reflection again.

Mrs Brennan suddenly stamped on the floor so hard she made me jump. It must have given the lift just the jolt it needed and once more it juddered into shaky life and continued its descent.

'Don't want you to be late for school, Fay,' she said, and grinned at me. She was wearing red lipstick that was spread beyond her mouth and had smudged on to her white false teeth. I tried to pretend I wasn't looking at that.

'Oh, I won't be late,' I said.

'Aye, but you were quite right yesterday. You're better using the stairs.'

We had almost reached the ground floor.

'Yesterday?'

'Aye, don't trust this blinking coffin of a thing. You've got young legs. Use the stairs.'

'I took the lift yesterday, Mrs Brennan.'

Young legs or not, I almost always used the lift.

The lift thumped to a halt at the bottom, and the doors creaked open. Mrs Brennan pulled her coat tight about her to face the cold morning air.

'I'm the one who is supposed to forget things, hen.

33

Yesterday. I saw ye going down the stairs while I was waiting for the lift.'

An icy finger was running down my spine.

'I remember thinking, what lovely hair. Bouncing above your collar it was, and I waved at you. Remember now?' She patted my cheek. 'And you waved back.'

34

CHAPTER SIX

I *was* late for school, and used the broken lift as an excuse. But actually I had dawdled, my mind racing with what Mrs Brennan had told me.

In the cold light of a November morning I shouldn't feel so afraid. And what was I afraid of exactly? I didn't even know. All I knew was that Mrs Brennan was mistaken. I had taken the lift yesterday; in fact, it had been almost a week since I'd clattered down all those flights of stairs, angry and annoyed that the odd lift had yet again broken down.

But yesterday. *No.*

'Your bonny hair bouncing above your collar,' she had said. And yesterday, I had indeed washed my hair. I remembered how much I had admired it myself as I looked in the lift mirror when I was going to school. How shiny it had been. Thinking how I must ask Mum

35

to buy that shampoo again.

But it wasn't me or my shiny hair that Mrs Brennan had seen. It wasn't me who had waved at her.

There had to be a logical explanation.

Memory loss.

That was a terrifying thought. My gran had once been as bright as a button. When she watched *Countdown* on TV every afternoon, she could do the sums quicker than anyone I knew. Yet, now, when we visited her in the nursing home she would ask me, 'Who are you? Do I know you?'

The first time it had happened I had thought she was playing a game with me, but when I realised that she really didn't recognise me I had cried so hard Mum couldn't comfort me. I hardly visited Gran now. She frightened me.

'It happens sometimes when you get old,' Mum had tried to explain.

But could it happen when you were young, like me? Was it hereditary? Did it run in our family?

I couldn't shake the thoughts from my mind all day.

'What is wrong with you, Fay?' Kaylie gave me a dunt.

'You've been in a dream all day.' Dawn looked at me with her eyes full of concern. 'Everything OK at home?'

Why did everyone always have to think it was something to do with home? 'Everything's fine at home,' I snapped at her. 'OK?'

Dawn sniffed with indignation. 'Keep your hair on. I'm trying to be nice here.'

I couldn't even bring myself to apologise to her. I wanted to explain, to talk about it with them. But what could I say that didn't sound daft? Anyway, I decided. It was probably just a stupid mistake that would never happen again.

Over the next few days it seemed that I was right. Nothing much happened at all. Except the nights got darker, and we were all caught up in Daft Donald's rehearsals for *Macbeth*.

Even our headmaster thought Donald was being a bit too ambitious.

'What about something more simple, Donald?' I heard him suggest one afternoon. '*Three Little Pigs*. This lot just might manage that one.' He guffawed with laughter at his joke.

What a cheek! *Three Little Pigs*, indeed.

Donald, however, was adamant. 'I want to stretch

them, push them to their limits. Help them to understand and appreciate the sheer poetry and drama of
Shakespeare.'

No wonder we called him Daft Donald.

Stretch us? I felt like yelling at him. He *was* stretch-
ing us, because this play was worse than the rack.

Especially for me. No matter how hard I tried I could
never seem to remember the lines. And every time I
stumbled over them, there was Monica at my elbow.

'Don't think I'm going to be understudy too long,'
she would say.

'You'll be fine, Fay,' Donald would say, coming over
to me and going over the lines with me again.

When Monica was out of earshot one afternoon I
asked him, 'Why exactly did you pick me, sir? I'm rubbish.' I whispered the last bit. Didn't want Monica to
know I agreed with her.

Donald shook his head. 'You are not rubbish, Fay.
Far from it. I think you've a quality that suits your
name. Fey. One minute I look at you and you're so
quiet and still, and the next, the anger just flashes out
and you can be quite scary. That's the quality I want you
to bring to the part.' He patted my shoulder. 'You'll be
fine, Fay,' he said again.

However, I wasn't the only one who was having bother. The three witches kept giggling, and Macduff kept tripping over his sword. After one disastrous readthrough Donald had had enough. He clapped his hands together to get our attention. 'Right, tomorrow after school you're all staying behind for an extra rehearsal.'

There was a communal groan.

'It'll be too dark, sir,' one of the boys shouted.

'We'll get the girls to see you home, to protect you,' Donald told him sarcastically.

'My mum won't let me stay behind,' one of the girls said.

He had an answer for that, too. 'Permission slips will be sent out to all the parents, or I'll phone personally. We'll arrange transport for those of you who can't get picked up afterwards. A door-to-door service.'

He glared around us. 'You really are a bunch of wimps,' he said.

Monica smirked at me. 'Well, some of us are anyway.'

I should have sniped back at her, 'You won't have to stay back, Monica. After all you're only the understudy. Who needs you?' But by the time I had thought of it she'd moved off with her friends, leaving me standing with a red face once again.

Drew Fraser was watching me and he shook his head and muttered as he passed me, 'Some Lady Macbeth!'

I'd show him, I thought. I was going to be so good at this rehearsal that I would shock them all.

And I did.

But it had nothing to do with the rehearsal.

CHAPTER SEVEN

Daft Donald spent the first half hour of the rehearsal doing his best to help us understand the plot of *Macbeth*.

'We know what it is, sir,' Drew Fraser shouted. 'Handsome king, mad wife.' He glanced at me and lifted an eyebrow. 'Some pantomime witches and a ghost . . . oh, and a couple of murders.'

Everyone laughed as if he had said something wildly funny. Everyone except me and Donald.

'Hey, Drew, you're making it sound interesting,' someone shouted.

'You've got to understand the mo-tiv-ation, Drew,' Donald spoke slowly and carefully as if Drew was an idiot. Which, of course, he was. 'If you understand the mo-tiv-ation of the characters, why they behave as they do, then you will understand the words . . . the beautiful words.'

It was the 'beautiful words' I had the most trouble with. Why couldn't they just talk like real people? All that wouldst, and shouldst. No wonder I could never remember what I was supposed to say.

When it came to my first scene I could tell Donald was getting fed up with me. And not only Donald. Monica kept chipping in: correcting me when I was wrong, cueing me when I hesitated.

'Shut your gob!' I wanted to yell at her.

Finally, Donald drew his hands through his hair in exasperation. 'Fay, honestly, this is Lady Macbeth's entrance. It's a really important scene.'

'It's an awfully long speech, sir,' I moaned. 'Could you not cut it down a bit?'

Monica sniggered behind me. 'If he cuts it down any more you'll be coming in and saying "Hi," and walking off.'

Once again everyone laughed. She was desperate to replace me. So she could show Donald what a wonderful Lady Macbeth she would make. That thought alone made me determined to try harder.

'I'll get it right, sir. I promise,' I assured him and he smiled.

'I'm sure you'll do your best.'

This caused another snigger from Monica and I heard Dawn snap at her, 'Jealousy's a terrible thing, Monica.'

Donald drew me aside. 'I'll tell you what, Fay. I have the video of *Macbeth* – it's in my briefcase in the staff room. You go and fetch it. Take it home and have a look at it. It might help you.'

As I left the auditorium he was calling out for the three witches to go over their scene with Macbeth and I could feel Monica's unsmiling eyes follow me even after I'd closed the door.

It was strange being in the school at night, in the dark. Strange and eerie. The lights from the auditorium shone into the corridor from its high windows, but apart from that the corridor was gloomy.

Gloomy and silent except for my footsteps, and the faraway sound of my classmates' voices. I pushed through the swing doors which led to the next corridor and as they swung to behind me I realised it was even darker in here. Far away, too far now for comfort, I could hear the rantings of the three witches, Dawn and Kaylie making the most of their parts. I stopped and glanced back. The doors swung back and forth, back and forth . . . almost as if someone had stepped through them a second behind me.

And all at once I was afraid again, and I didn't know why.

I was in my own school. I spent almost every day here. Nothing to be afraid of here. Yet, I watched mesmerised as the doors swung back and forth as if I was waiting for—

Nonsense! I stamped my foot. I was just being silly. I will not be afraid, I told myself. And I turned round, saw it, and screamed.

How stupid can one person be? It was only my reflection. A dark image on a classroom window. I let out my breath in a long relieved sigh. Light. I needed light. There would be nothing to be afraid of in the light. I found the switches and threw them on. A long string of lights beamed down the corridor to the staffroom. Better. So much better. My steps even sounded more confident as I clicked along.

In the staffroom, I immediately switched on the light there too.

Donald's battered leather briefcase lay half open on the floor. I lifted it up and held it against me. Nothing strange here, I told myself, looking round at the posters on the wall. Mel Gibson, and Homer Simpson, a cartoon of the headmaster. Not unlike the posters we all kept in our lockers. Ordinary, safe, normal.

Suddenly, the light went out, plunging the staffroom into darkness. A blown light bulb, I told myself, refusing to be frightened. I took a step back into the corridor and closed the door.

I had only taken one step towards the swing doors when the light above me went out too.

One bulb, that could be an accident, but two? I ran as I passed beneath the next light.

It went out, too.

And the next.

Now, I *was* frightened. What was happening?

I ran, breathing hard. Above me, the next dim light was extinguished. My breath began to catch. I was really afraid now, because surely I could hear footsteps behind me. I glanced back quickly but all was pitch dark, a tunnel of blackness reaching down the corridor.

Nothing.

And yet . . . wasn't that a movement? There in the shadows. Something. I didn't want to find out what. I ran even faster, feeling as if the darkness itself was chasing me as, one after another, each light went out above me.

Then I heard them. No mistaking it now. Footsteps were coming up behind me in the blackness.

I had to reach the swing doors. Beyond them was light, the school auditorium, other people.

It was as if I was in a dream, a nightmare. Running but getting nowhere. As if the swing doors were moving further and further away. Too afraid to glance back, too afraid that those footsteps would catch up with me.

They were closing in on me, coming nearer and nearer. I was sure I could feel something, a hand almost brushing against my back. I threw myself forward. It mustn't touch me. Somehow, I knew I mustn't let it touch me.

Fear got the better of me. I couldn't take it anymore, and I screamed. I screamed at the top of my voice.

'Help me! Somebody help me!'

I fell through the swing doors and landed in a heap, scattering the contents of Donald's briefcase everywhere.

The corridor was suddenly filled with people swarming out of the auditorium. Kaylie and Dawn were there first. They looked shocked when they saw me, lying breathlessly against the wall, crying. I pointed to the darkened corridor, beyond the still swinging doors. 'There. In there,' I gasped.

They looked baffled.

'Someone's after me. The lights all went out. They were behind me.'

'Who was?' Dawn asked.

I shook my head, as baffled as they were. 'I don't know. Somebody. I was so scared.'

The swing doors flew open again. I covered my face with my hands, and let out a yell. I was afraid to look.

'Who's been tampering wi' my lights?' It was Mr Gray, the school janitor. He thought the school was his private property.

My words came out in a sob when I answered him. 'I didn't touch your lights.' I peered behind him into the shadows. 'Someone was after me.'

'Aye! Me!' he snapped, and his attention turned to Donald, who was standing watching me. 'Are you lot nearly finished in here?'

Donald looked at me with something close to annoyance. 'Yes, Mr Gray. I think we'll be calling it a night quite soon.'

I wanted to make him understand. 'It wasn't Mr Gray who was after me, sir. It was someone else.'

'It was only your imagination, Fay,' Donald said softly.

Why wouldn't anyone believe me? Why were they looking at me as if I had made it all up? I yelled back at him: 'It wasn't my imagination. Somebody was running after me . . . and it wasn't him!' I jabbed a finger towards the janitor.

Donald patted me on the shoulder. 'There, there, calm down, Fay.' He said it as if I was a bad-tempered little girl. I could have screamed at him.

'What's all this commotion?' Monica stepped out of the girls' toilets behind me. She took the situation in and sneered at me. 'You causing more trouble? Like to be the centre of attention now, don't you?' She pushed past me in disgust and strode back to the auditorium.

'How long was she in the toilets?' I asked Kaylie.

She shrugged. 'Ages. Left just after you . . . takes her that long to make herself beautiful.'

Dawn laughed, wanted me to laugh too. But I couldn't. I was still shaking.

'What I don't understand is,' Kaylie said, 'if you were so scared why did you go back down the corridor?'

Something in me shivered. 'What do you mean, go back down the corridor?'

'You stood at the door of the theatre, and just stood

48

there staring into space . . . as if you were in a dream.'

'Yes,' Dawn tutted. 'You didn't even answer me when I called to you. You just turned round and went back down the corridor. I thought you must have forgotten something.'

Now I was shaking. Shaking so hard I couldn't stop. 'No, no! That wasn't me.'

I was beginning to annoy my friends. 'Of course it was you, Fay.'

'Are you trying to make out we're daft, or something?'

Suddenly, I was yelling again, yelling so loudly I could have awakened the dead. Everyone stopped to stare at me. Monica turned and just looked, with a satisfied smirk on her face.

'That wasn't me!' I screamed at them. 'That wasn't me!'

CHAPTER EIGHT

My outburst finished any possibility of continuing the rehearsal. Donald wound the whole thing up and sat with me until Dad came to collect me. 'Would you like to speak to Mrs Williams, the school counsellor?' he asked while we waited.

I snapped out my answer. 'No! I wouldn't.'

Donald and his like thought the answer to everything was in counselling. I did want to talk to someone, but only so they could explain what was happening. But how could they? It sounded crazy even to me.

Drew Fraser came up to me before he left. 'Well, Lady Macbeth does go mad. Is this you building up to that, or what?'

'That's enough, Drew!' Donald scolded him angrily. 'Fay's had a bit of a fright, that's all.'

Drew shrugged his shoulders and went off sniggering, surrounded by his adoring fans – one of whom was Monica.

Dad looked really concerned when he saw me. I had stopped crying, but my eyes were red-rimmed. 'I got a real fright,' I explained to him. 'I thought someone was coming after me in the corridor.'

Now he really was worried. 'And was there?'

Yes, there was, I wanted to say. Someone waiting in the shadows, watching me, laughing at my fear. But how could I explain it, even to him?

'It was the janny,' I said finally.

He breathed a sigh of relief.

'But Dad, funny things have been happening over the past few days. Things I don't understand,' I said on the way home in the car. 'People keep saying they saw me, but I wasn't there. It wasn't me they saw.'

He glanced at me, taking his eyes off the road for just a second. 'Mistakes happen. Somebody told me only last week they saw me in town. Wasn't me. I was fixing a woman's washing machine in Airdrie at the time.' He smiled. 'Everybody's got a double they say.'

But tonight, I thought, in the school, my two best friends had seen someone, and were sure that some-one was me. And they wouldn't make a mistake like that, would they?

Dad had turned his eyes back to the road, and now his voice was bitter. 'Happens to your mother all the time. People tell me they see her somewhere, but she always insists it wasn't her. Couldn't possibly be her.' He glanced at me again. 'So she must have a double as well, eh?'

It was always the same. Everything came back to them, him and Mum. How could I ask him to help me understand now? I was better shutting up. I would try to work it out myself. It would never happen again. I wouldn't let it.

I turned and looked out the window. It was so dark all I could see was my own tearful reflection.

How did I feel that night?

As if I was on a train hurtling through the dark on a collision course. I couldn't get off no matter how I tried.

And I was the only passenger.

CHAPTER NINE

'Are you feeling better?' Mum asked next morning as I was leaving for school. She had sat up with me late into the night, listening to me and trying to explain in the best way she could what had happened. I had told her as much as I had told Dad, and her response had been the same as his. People make mistakes. Everyone has a double somewhere. In the dimly lit corridor, she assured me, I had let my imagination take over. All sensible, common-sense explanations, but none of them had helped me sleep.

Yet, this morning, I did feel better. Here, today, with a frosty sun hovering low in the sky and Kaylie and Dawn waiting for me at the top of the stairs, the fears of last night seemed stupid, unreal. There was a logical explanation for all this. There had to be.

And all that day, nothing happened. I apologised to

Donald and he patted me on the head as if I was a pet poodle. 'Just know your lines for the next rehearsal,' he said. 'That's all I ask.'

Yet, as the day wore on, the dark feeling settled on me again, like a shroud being laid around my shoulders.

'I think I'll take the long road home today,' I told the girls as we stood chatting at the top of the stairs. I was looking down them as the midwinter dusk was falling. In the dim lights, the bare branches of the trees that hung over the wall were like bony fingers ready to reach out and touch me. The very thought made me shiver.

'Kaylie and I will come down the stairs with you, if you like,' Dawn offered.

But I shook my head. I couldn't face those stairs today, though I wasn't going to admit that to them.

'No, honestly, I just feel like the walk. I'm going over my lines in my head, you see.' How they couldn't see that for what it was, a blatant lie, I do not know. They let me go, however, and stood watching me as if I was an infant heading off for her first day at school.

I turned the corner, and disappeared behind a row of houses, but as I emerged between them and looked round, there were my two friends, still watching me. Dawn waved. So did Kaylie, and I hurried on, trying not to get annoyed at them. They were worried about me, I told myself, and I was touched by their concern. I was lucky to have such good friends.

The men were fixing the odd lift when I went into our block. Or rather, they were sitting inside it drinking mugs of tea. GALWAY COUNTY LIBRARIES

'Sorry, darlin',' one of them said and winked at me, 'you'll have to use the even lift today.'

'Or else walk up the stairs,' suggested the other.

My reflection in the steel at the back of the odd lift made me realise just how pale I was. I needed to get my circulation going to give myself a bit of colour, so I headed for the stairs.

I was more out of condition than I thought, because I was panting by the time I hurried into the flat. The phone was ringing in the hall and I just made it in time. The mirror on the wall showed me I had colour now. My face was red and damp with sweat and my ribs were aching.

'Hello?' I was breathless. 'Who's this?'

Dawn sounded worried. 'What's wrong? What happened?'

I giggled. 'I'm not fit. I've just walked up thirteen

flights of stairs and I'm about dead.'

Dawn let out a sigh of relief. 'You gave me such a fright there. Me and Kaylie are just checking up you got home all right.'

Annoyance nipped at me again, but I pushed it away. 'Honestly, what are you two like!'

Kaylie piped up. I could imagine her yanking the phone from Dawn. 'You did see us waving at you?' There was an embarrassed hesitation. 'Remember? When you went between that block of houses. You waved back? Didn't you?'

I didn't say anything for a moment, and this time I didn't push the annoyance aside. 'Do you think I'm daft, is that it? Do you think I'm going crazy?'

Dawn tried to explain, but I wouldn't let her.

'Yes, it was me!' I yelled. 'This time it *was* me. I remember. I saw you. I waved back. OK?'

And I slammed down the phone.

CHAPTER TEN

'I don't think I like this Lady Macbeth very much,' I said, slamming the book shut. 'She's a nag. She's horrible. She wants her husband to murder somebody.'

We were in the canteen with another rehearsal looming tonight, and Kaylie and Dawn were doing their best to help me remember my lines. Unsuccessfully.

Dawn sucked milk noisily through a straw. 'She's a very strong woman, Fay.'

But I couldn't see that at all. Did you have to be so nasty to be strong? Surely not. I wasn't nasty. Did that make me weak?

We suddenly heard Monica's loud giggle from the far corner of the canteen. She was sitting on a table, waving her arms around, and whatever she had just told her friends had sent them into fits of laughter.

'Now, there's a perfect Lady Macbeth,' I muttered.

Kaylie punched me. 'No, she is not. You are not going to let old Moaning Minnie Monica get this part.'

I sighed. 'It's not a contest. I don't care.'

Dawn gave me a hug. 'Yes, you do care. You don't want her to get the better of you either.'

They were right of course. For that reason alone I would battle on with the play. What was the point of arguing? I couldn't let my two friends down.

'We're going to help you with the lines . . . even if it means tattooing them all over your body.'

That sent us all into the giggles.

Suddenly, Kaylie snatched the book from me. 'And gorgeous Drew is your husband. Let me see. Is there any kissing in this play?'

In spite of all their help, that night at the rehearsal, I was awful, and there were some rather rude words I'd rather not have remembered in front of the boys.

Whenever I blushed, Monica would let out a scream. 'Twenty-first-century woman! Ha! Nowadays we're supposed to be as bold as any man! Not get embarrassed at the slightest thing.'

I wanted to yell at her. I'd heard Monica swear in the corridor. She thought it impressed people. She thought being a twenty-first-century woman meant doing every horrible thing that boys do. Only doing them more often, and worse. So nothing would embarrass her.

Even I had to admit that Drew made an impressive Macbeth. His voice had broken already and it boomed out through the auditorium. And he told Donald he intended to wear a kilt when the play actually went on. Every girl listening swooned when he said that. Every girl except me. But Drew Fraser in a kilt? That would send the female hearts in the audience beating so fast it wouldn't matter if he didn't say a word.

Kaylie sighed. 'Drew Fraser in a kilt? I'll die, so I will.'

'If somebody shouts up from the audience, "What do you see in that wimp, Macbeth?" I'll be the one who'll just die,' I said.

'You'll have to do something about that self-esteem of yours, Fay,' Dawn said. They were both enjoying every minute of the whole thing. Revelling in their parts as the witches, screaming whenever Drew Fraser stepped on stage. Enjoying Monica's jealousy of me. I wished I could be more like them. They never seemed to worry about anything. But, of course, they didn't have to stand up on the stage on their own, with every eye on them.

No, I couldn't call it fun.

'Your dad coming for you tonight?' Kaylie asked me.

'Not tonight. He's working late, but Donald said he'd give me a lift home.'

Dawn gave me a push. 'You're not going home with a teacher. My mum's coming for me. She can give you a lift.'

Dawn's mum had us laughing all the way home. Just back from Weightwatchers, she'd put on three pounds and she did nothing but rant and rave that the 'blinking scales were off', or maybe she'd 'worn too much make-up'.

'I starved myself for a week, and I put on three pounds! That's not possible! I only ever eat half a doughnut!'

I was still laughing when they dropped me off at the flats. Especially since Dawn's mum had decided to take them for a fish and chip supper as a consolation.

'What the hell,' she bawled. 'The diet's not working anyway!'

Dawn always seemed to have so much fun with her family. I was almost jealous of her.

The odd lift was actually working for once but as I

hurried into the entrance I could hear the machinery whirr into life and hear the doors creaking as they began to close.

'Hold it! Please!' I shouted.

I broke into a run, but I didn't make it and in the second the doors slid closed I caught a glimpse of my reflection in the mirrored steel at the back of the lift.

Now I would have to wait until the lift came down again. I watched its progress in the lighted numbers above the doors.

7-9-11-13.

It came to a halt at my floor. Someone getting in? Someone getting out?

The doors of the even lift opened and one of our neighbours stepped out. 'Oh, is that one actually working?'

I nodded, noticing that the lift had begun its descent again. 13-11 . . .

'Makes a change, doesn't it?' I said.

'I wouldn't trust it, hen. The men have been working on it all day. Sure you don't want to go up in this one?'

But even if I'd wanted to, the doors had begun to close as the lift was summoned by someone on another floor.

9-7-5.

'No. I'll take the chance,' I said, laughing as I remembered Dawn's mum and her diet.

The neighbour went off muttering. 'We want to do something about that lift. It needs to be totally renewed. Or, better still, the council needs to be renewed.'

3-1.

The odd lift arrived and the doors slid open. I hesitated, half expecting someone to step out. The someone who had perhaps got in at my floor. But the lift was empty. Someone must have got out at my floor.

I stepped inside, and pressed 13. The doors creaked shut and the lift began to rise, trundling almost painfully, floor by floor. Doesn't sound too healthy, I thought, hoping it would hold out, at least until it reached the thirteenth floor again.

It was then that something struck me as odd. Do you ever get a feeling like that? There was something that, for a moment, I couldn't put my finger on.

Something strange and out of place.

Something about the lift.

Something—

Suddenly, I thought I knew what it was.

My heart began to thump like a drum. My spine turned to ice. I began to turn around, ever so slowly.

The shock of what I saw took my breath away.

No, it wasn't what I saw. It was what I didn't see.

I didn't see *me*!

I should have been looking at my reflection staring back at me. Instead, there were only breeze blocks and girders. And a sign.

WE REGRET ANY INCONVENIENCE CAUSED BY REPAIRS TO THIS LIFT.

The stainless steel mirror was gone.

But only minutes ago I had glimpsed my reflection in it.

Hadn't I?

Or had I, for the very first time, glimpsed the other one?

CHAPTER ELEVEN

What was happening? It couldn't be true. *Couldn't.* I went over in my head exactly what I'd seen. My reflection staring back at me as the lift doors were sliding shut.

My reflection.

Same clothes. Same hair. Same surprised expression.

Yet . . .

It couldn't have been my reflection. There was no mirrored steel wall at the back of the lift. Only the workmen's sign, and brick wall of the lift well behind it.

So, what had I seen?

Who?

Me?

No. That was madness. Crazy thought.

Yet, people were seeing me, where I wasn't. It was happening too often to be coincidence. All this was beginning to make me really afraid.

And then, another terrifying thought hit me.

Where had this other one gone to?

The lift had stopped at level 13. My floor! No one had got in. So, someone must have got out! The *someone* whose image I had seen? Was that someone, even now, waiting up there? Waiting for the lift doors to open?

Waiting for me?

I watched as the lift rose steadily upwards. The ninth floor. The eleventh.

Almost there.

I was breathing so fast it hurt.

Waiting for me? And then what? Suddenly, I didn't want to know. I didn't want to find out. I jabbed my fingers at the buttons.

EMERGENCY STOP!

But it didn't stop. It wouldn't.

For once, the odd lift wouldn't stop.

13.

I was here. And I had never been so afraid in all my life.

I pressed myself back against the side of the lift as the doors creaked their way open. If I could have melted into the concrete I would have.

What was waiting for me on the thirteenth floor?

Nothing.

The doors slid open, and stood silent waiting for me to step out.

No one was there. Still breathing hard, I took one tentative step forward, hardly daring to look . . . to my left . . . to my right.

My heart jumped as I glimpsed a shadow! Coming round the corner. Rushing towards me. Someone *was* here!

I closed my eyes and screamed. I screamed as loud and as long as I could. Screamed even louder as someone grabbed me, their fingers biting into my shoulders.

Doors were pulled open. Every neighbour we had ran from their flat. They flooded on to the landing. Including my mother. She was the first person I saw when I finally opened my eyes. In her dressing gown, her hair just washed, panic etched on her face.

The second was Mr Reynolds, our other next-door neighbour. He was the one holding my shoulders and trying to calm me down.

'I'm sorry, love. Did I frighten you?' He glanced at my mother apologetically. 'I rang for the lift and then went back to check I'd locked the door. She was getting out just as I turned the corner. I must have frightened the life out of the wee lassie.'

I could see that some of our other neighbours weren't so understanding.

'I thought somebody was getting murdered,' I heard one of them complain.

'I'm . . . I'm sorry,' I stammered. I looked at Mum. 'I'm sorry.'

She was apologising, too, for me. Looking around the neighbours, trying to get them to understand. 'It's because it's so late, and the landing's so dark. Sorry.'

When Mr Reynolds went off in the lift, and the neighbours had closed their doors again, satisfied but perhaps a little disappointed there hadn't been a murder, my mother led me inside the house. 'My goodness, Fay, that was a bit OTT just because a neighbour darted round the corner to catch the lift.'

I wanted to confide in her. I suppose I wanted someone to explain it all away logically so I could understand. But not to my mum. Not then. Because even then I could sense an icy atmosphere in the house. Dad was in the kitchen eating his dinner as if it had been poisoned. And Mum began banging dishes about angrily.

They'd had another argument.

The last thing they needed was for me to ask them to explain what was happening to me.

I didn't sleep well that night. But by next morning I had made a decision. I would confide in Kaylie and Dawn. They seemed my only hope. My best friends. Who else could I trust? Even though I knew when I told them they would think I was even loopier than they had thought before.

They listened, Dawn with her mouth open and her eyes wide like saucers. Kaylie with a milk-lined grin. I told them everything, finishing with the apparition (if that's what it was) in the lift.

Dawn shivered. 'That's dead creepy,' she said, excited.

Kaylie sounded annoyed. 'I thought you didn't like ghost stories?'

Why couldn't she understand? 'It's not a ghost story,' I told her. 'It really happened. I want you to help me find a logical explanation.'

A logical explanation was the last thing they wanted. But it was Dawn who came up with one.

'Have you ever thought you might have a twin? An

identical twin?'

I must have gone pale for Kaylie pulled me close. 'Are you all right? Do you think that might be the answer?'

'But, why would my mum and dad keep me, and give away my twin?'

Dawn couldn't meet my eyes. 'Maybe your mum kept a lot of secrets from you.'

She was talking about my mum's secret boyfriend. Hinting that if a mum could have a boyfriend, what was to stop her having other secrets?

I shook my head. 'No. I don't believe that.'

Dawn didn't let it go. 'Well, maybe not a twin. But a sister. A sister so like you no one can tell the difference. Maybe your mum had her before—' She almost said, 'before she was married.' But she blushed and just said, 'It could happen.'

A sister.

'Maybe she's just found out about you, and she's jealous because she was given up for adoption and now she thinks you've got her life.'

'And she wants it back,' Dawn finished.

A sister. Was that the explanation?

I thought about it all that day, not knowing if it was

better than the alternative. But I knew I had to find out. I had to know the truth.

That night, I waited for the right moment to confront Mum. My eyes didn't leave her all the while we sat in front of the TV. Watching her, wondering if she really had given my sister away and if that sister was back now, watching *me*.

When Dad went in for his bath she turned to me and asked, 'Is something bothering you, Fay?'

I wet my lips nervously. 'Mum, have you got any secrets you haven't told me?'

Her face grew stern. 'I don't have secrets any more. Right!' She nodded towards the bathroom. 'Has he put you up to this? Is he telling you I'm still seeing—' she blushed. 'I go to work. I come home. I don't even go out with my friends. No secrets. Not any more.'

I shook my head. 'I didn't mean that. Honest, Mum. I meant . . . a long time ago. Before I was born.' I was trying to find the right words. Not making a very good job of it. 'Have you ever had another baby?'

Her face crumpled into a relieved smile. She was suddenly on the sofa next to me. Hugging me close. 'You know I lost two babies before you. I am so lucky to have you. My only precious baby.' She kissed my brow.

Normally I would be dead embarrassed if she did that, but now it comforted me. It felt good to be hugged.

'Now, what brought that on?' she asked.

'People keep seeing someone who looks like me. They think it is me. She seems to be following me. I thought maybe . . .' I let the words drift into the silence.

'You thought you had a sister somewhere? A daughter I'd given up before you were born?' She shook her head. 'You read too many books. This girl probably doesn't look a bit like you really. Not half as pretty. She'll be jealous of you, I bet.' She pulled me to my feet. 'Come on. Let's make some cheese on toast for supper. We'll have it ready for Dad when he comes out of his bath. Give him a treat.'

I knew it wasn't a satisfactory explanation, but I pushed it away, refusing to think of it anymore. Because this was what I loved best. Me and Mum and Dad, sitting round the table eating cheese on toast, just like old times.

I decided that night would be the end of it. It would never happen again.

CHAPTER TWELVE

'So, no sister?' Dawn sounded disappointed.

Kaylie was still determined that a sister had to be the explanation. 'What about your dad? Did you ask him?'

'I think Mum would know if she'd had another baby.'

Kaylie tutted. 'I don't mean your mum's baby, silly. I mean . . . maybe your dad had a girlfriend, and she had a baby. A girl. Same age as you. And now she's stalking you, because you're the one with the dad.'

She really did have some imagination. 'You watch too many soaps, Kaylie. This is real life, remember.'

'Truth,' she said, with a sniff, 'is stranger than fiction.'

I dismissed her suggestion. 'Even if that *was* true, she wouldn't look so much like me. I don't look like Dad at all.' I looked just like Mum. Same fair hair, same turned-up nose, same smile. Her mirror image, people who had known her as a girl would say.

'Well, I've run out of ideas then,' Dawn said. 'Are you sure you're not just potty?' She grinned at me, and Kaylie giggled. So did I. Not letting them see how scary that suggestion actually was.

I was hardly listening as Mr Hardie the science teacher droned on. It was not my favourite subject, and I had another rehearsal tonight. Under the desk I had my *Macbeth* script open and was trying to memorise the lines.

Suddenly, I was given a dunt that almost sent me flying off my seat. I looked up and Dawn was mouthing at me, wide-eyed, urging me to listen to the teacher. I looked up at him, baffled, and then I did listen. As I realised what he was talking about, my eyes went as wide as Dawn's.

Clones.

He was talking about clones.

How, by taking a simple DNA sample from one creature we now had the technology to copy that creature exactly.

Hair by hair, bone by bone, cell by cell.

'Can they do it with human beings, sir?' I called out,

interrupting him and taking the whole class by surprise. Taking myself by surprise too. I was thinking aloud.

Mr Hardie blinked, surprised too by my interest. 'In the realms of science fiction, yes. They've been cloning people for years in movies. But so far, in real life, it's never been done.'

'As far as you know?' I said.

There was a giggle from the back of the class. Monica. 'Maybe that's the answer, Fay. You've been cloned.' She laughed like a horse and explained to the teacher. 'You see, sir, our Fay here, keeps thinking somebody's impersonating her. Pretending to be her. As if one of her wasn't enough.' She made a face at me when she said that. I swear if she'd been sitting close to me I would have slapped her. 'Do you think that's the answer, sir? Has she been cloned?'

Mr Hardie answered kindly. 'Probably there is a much more mundane explanation. Mistaken identity, Fay. Happens all the time. That's why the reliability of eye witness identification is being called into question.'

He smiled at me. But I had to know more, in spite of the amusement I was causing for Monica and her friends. 'But, sir, if they could actually clone human beings, could you ever tell the difference?'

He sat up on his desk. 'Let's put it this way, Fay. If I was to clone you, no one could tell the difference. Not at first. But if your clone wore different clothes, cut her hair in a different style, or dyed it a different colour, if she started developing different habits to you, smoking, biting her nails. You'd soon hardly see the resemblance. Do you understand?'

I thought I did. A clone was only your mirror image in those first few seconds of creation. After that, it took on its own identity, became its own person.

As we sat in the auditorium for rehearsals that night Monica couldn't resist having another go at me. 'You really are pathetic. Clones! Do you realise how stupid you sounded?'

'What is all this anyway?' Drew Fraser came over and joined in. 'I'm really fascinated by the idea of clones. I'm always looking up things like that on the Internet.' He was staring at me as if for the first time. 'I mean . . . are you the real Fay, or the clone? And how would I know which was which?'

I was sure he was making a fool of me. 'Stop talking as if I was someone out of one of your stupid horror films!'

'I'm trying to be serious for once. I really am interested.'

Of course I didn't believe that. I knew Drew Fraser too well.

'Anyway, why would you care!' I snapped at him, and began to push past him.

'Because I'm your husband, Lady Macbeth! It's my business to know!' he shouted after me, and that had everybody laughing.

Everybody except me, and Monica. I could hear her say loudly to Drew, 'It would be easy to tell which was which, Drew, son. The clone would be the one who could remember the lines.'

CHAPTER THIRTEEN

Now, another idea had taken hold. Clones. Was that the answer? Had I been cloned without even knowing it?

I decided that as soon as I had the chance I would raid the library, read everything I could about cloning and find out more.

Next morning I left for school after Mum and Dad had gone off to work. In the hall I looked at myself in the mirror, at my shiny fair hair, at my bright blue eyes. It was hard to believe there was another, somewhere, just like me. Exactly like me. Almost impossible to believe.

But it had to be true. There was no other explanation.

As I came out of our house the door leading to the stairs was just banging shut. I could hear footsteps on the landing. Oh no, I thought, please don't let the lift be broken again!

But to my relief there was Mrs Brennan, waiting patiently. It was Tuesday, her pension day.

'The lift's definitely working?' I asked her.

She pursed her lips. 'Oh, talking to me now are you? I've just told you the lift was working and you ignored me. In this day and age manners seem to be a thing of the past.'

I grew cold. 'You told me—? When?'

She looked annoyed now. 'Just now.' She pointed a finger to the stairway doors. 'Did you change your mind about going down the stairs?'

Just now. Going down the stairs.

I had seen the door banging shut. Heard the footsteps.

Her. The other one.

I gasped. That must mean . . . *she* was there now, on the stairs.

Mrs Brennan stepped towards me. 'What's the matter, hen? You've gone as white as death.'

But already I was turning away from her, ignoring her. This time, if I ran, I would catch her. I was going to find out the truth.

I hauled open the door to the stairs and listened.

Clip-clip-clip. Feet on the stairs, tapping out their descent. Shoes just like mine.

I stepped on to the landing and looked over the railing. From here I could see all thirteen floors spiralling down through the gloomy stairwell.

My heart went into overdrive. There was a hand on the stair railing, only two floors down. A girl's hand. A hand like mine. I jumped back, in that second afraid of what I might come face to face with. But only for a second. It had to be confronted. This had to be finished. Here in the echoing stairwell was surely better than a pitch black school corridor at night.

All at once, I was running, my feet clattering wildly on the stairs. Floor by floor. Flight by flight. Swinging myself round on each landing. Faster and faster. As I speeded up, it seemed so did she.

At the ninth floor I stopped suddenly, my hand poised on the railing. I glanced down. She had stopped too. This other one, and I could see her delicate hand on the railing exactly as mine was. It took all my courage to call out to her.

'Who are you? Why are you doing this to me?'

As I waited for her answer I felt as if my heart had stopped beating.

'Who are you?' I screamed again.

It seemed to me I heard a muffled giggle. Was it my imagination, or was she laughing at me?

Whatever it was it made me angry and my anger spurred me on. I ran faster than ever down the stairs though my legs were aching, and I could feel the blood pounding in my temples. But I would catch her. I had to.

Yet, no matter how fast I ran, she ran every bit as fast.

I stopped again at the fourth floor for only a second, and glanced down. Was she closer now? Was I catching up with her? This time I didn't call out. I wasn't going to waste my breath. I ran even faster.

Down and down.

Still I couldn't catch her.

'Stop!' I yelled breathlessly. 'Stop! Let me see you.'

I was so afraid I was going to miss her again.

Knew that I was.

I heard her feet on the last step, saw the sunlight flood in as the street door was pushed open. Heard her footsteps echoing into the distance as they hurried into the street.

I was only seconds behind her, only seconds pushing through into the street. I was almost in tears. She must be somewhere close.

The street was busy. Pupils just like me hurrying to school. Mothers pushing toddlers in prams towards the shops. Pensioners heading for the post office.

I grabbed an elderly woman standing right outside. 'Did you see her? Did you?'

The woman, a cigarette dangling from her lips, snarled at me. 'See who?'

'A girl like me, coming out of there.' I pointed at the doors. 'You must have seen her. She must have run past you.'

The woman answered gruffly, 'I never saw nobody, right?'

Mrs Brennan appeared from the entrance to the flats. I ran to her. 'Mrs Brennan, that wasn't me you saw up there. It was somebody else.'

But she wouldn't believe me either. ''Course it was you. I'd recognise you anywhere.' She flicked at my hair with affection. 'Could never mistake that lovely bouncy hair of yours.'

No one would ever believe me.

But then I realised what I had to do. 'Well, you'll never make that mistake again!' I screamed at her.

I ran for the lift, and punched at the buttons angrily. Again, my anger was replacing my fear and when I reached my floor I flew out of the lift and into the flat. I made straight for the bathroom and stared at myself in the mirror.

At me.

Not this other one.

ME!

I lifted the scissors Mum kept in the cabinet above the sink.

No one would ever mistake her for me again.

CHAPTER FOURTEEN

'What have you done to your hair!' Dawn and Kaylie looked horrified when I came running into the playground during morning break. Horrifed that my soft, golden hair now stood out in spikey, unsightly tufts on my head. I had cut it. I had chopped it. I put up my hand to flatten it down, but it just kept springing up again.

Kaylie came over and hugged me. 'What have you done?' she said again.

'I saw her,' I began, then, remembering I hadn't actually seen her, I corrected myself. 'I *almost* saw her. Almost caught her. Mrs Brennan saw her. She spoke to her. She thought it was me.'

Dawn tutted. 'She's an old bag. Blind as a bat. She was probably just mistaken.'

I turned on her angrily. 'Everybody can't be

mistaken. There *is* somebody else.'

They were looking at me as if they didn't know me, almost as if they were afraid of me.

'What's happening to you, Fay?' Kaylie asked.

I touched my hair. 'You remember what Mr Hardie was saying about clones? Well, I've changed my hair. Her hair is soft and shiny, but mine isn't anymore. Now nobody – nobody! – will mistake her for me again.'

Drew Fraser stepped from behind a corner of the playground. He had been listening. 'Well, there's no chance of two girls having a haircut from hell like that.'

I pushed him so hard he almost stumbled. 'Shut up you!'

'Fay. Come to my office right now.' Mrs Williams' voice behind me was brisk and angry. She led me silently, with clipped heels and a tight mouth, to her office. She didn't say a word until I'd sat down and she'd closed the door. 'Now, Fay. You're late. Why?'

I couldn't tell her the truth. She wouldn't understand. So the lie came easily. 'I was stuck in the lift. I'm sorry, Mrs Williams.'

The problems with our lift were notorious but I still don't think she believed me.

'And this?' She flicked a tuft of my hair. 'Were you

stuck in the lift with a pair of shears?'

That was more difficult to explain, so this time I didn't try. 'There's someone pretending to be me, Mrs Williams. People keep seeing her. They think it's me. So I thought . . . if I cut my hair we'd look different. She wouldn't be mistaken for me again.'

She looked bewildered. Wondering why someone being mistaken for you should call for such drastic action. 'Yes, I've heard you've been saying that.' As if I was making it up. 'Fay, would you like to talk about this?'

I was on my feet in a second. 'Why? Because I'm late for school? Because I cut my hair? Does that mean I'm potty?'

She sighed. 'You know it's more than that. It's your behaviour lately. A few of the teachers have commented on it.'

I wanted to go quickly. Before she started on about my home life, my mum's boyfriend. Was that all they ever thought about? I straightened up and smiled. 'You'll see, Mrs Williams. I'll be OK from now on. I promise. Can I go now, please?'

She saw there was no holding me. 'You know if you ever need me, I'll be here. OK, Fay?'

'OK.' I agreed at once. Then I was out of that office and racing down the corridor to my class.

In spite of all the jibes – and there were plenty, especially from Monica – I forgot about my hair. I felt so much better. I had solved it. I had made myself look different. Now, no one would ever get us mixed up again.

However, I still had my mother to face.

She went white when she saw me. 'Fay. Your lovely hair.' Her eyes filled up with tears. 'Why did you do that?'

I told her. What was the point of lying to my mum? I told her that this other one had been on the stairs today and that it was beginning to really frighten me.

'She was the reason you asked if you had a sister?'

I nodded, and she smiled. 'I can assure you, you haven't got a clone either, Fay. They don't exist. I know you find it hard to believe but there will be a perfectly logical explanation. Mistaken identity. Or someone who looks like you is playing a cruel practical joke.'

'That's what Dad said.'

Her face fell. 'So, he was told the whole story first, I suppose?'

There was a time, I thought, when they would have confided in each other. We were a threesome. Now it

86

seemed we each lived in our own separate worlds.

Suddenly, she seemed to brighten. 'Well, I will tell you this, young lady. You're not going back to school looking like that.'

Now I brightened. 'Ever again?' I asked hopefully.

She was grinning as she lifted the phone and began to dial. 'I'm going to call my pal, Stella. The hairdresser. Remember her?'

Stella, who owned her own shop in town, wore too much make-up, smoked too much, and smelled of too many different perfumes. I liked her.

'How could I forget Stella?'

Mum was about to say something else when the phone was answered. She shook her finger at me to keep quiet. 'Is that you, Stella? Hi, it's Rona. I know, I've not seen you for ages. Well, I'm phoning for a favour. You remember my daughter, Fay?' There was a pause. Stella obviously remembered. 'Could I possibly bring her over to your house tonight? She really needs a major makeover with her hair.'

CHAPTER FIFTEEN

It didn't look a bit like me staring back from the mirror.

Stella stood beside Mum, her arms folded, surveying her handiwork with satisfaction.

'Would you believe the difference it makes!' she said. 'You look so grown up, Fay.'

I could hardly believe it myself. The clumps and tufts had been cut away and my hair had been layered into the back of my head, and the top was spikey and tousled.

Mum was delighted too. 'It looks so modern. It makes you look . . .' She searched around for the right word. 'Elfin.'

I wasn't quite sure what that meant, but I knew it was a compliment. When Stella's daughter arrived home with her boyfriend she raved about my hair too.

As we sat around Stella's kitchen table drinking tea and chatting, I kept sneaking quick glances at myself in the mirror, as delighted as everyone else.

How I loved that night. Mum and Stella and her daughter and me. Laughing and talking and having fun.

'A real girls' night!' Stella said, ignoring her daughter's poor boyfriend in the other room.

A real girls' night. If Mum left, I would lose nights like this, and I couldn't bear that.

But I wouldn't lose them. Mum would never leave.

When we went home Dad was even more impressed with my new hairstyle. 'That is lovely!' He looked at Mum. 'Was this your idea?'

He wanted it to be her idea, pleased to see us together like this.

'Of course it was her idea,' I said at once. Then I went over every detail of our night at Stella's.

This was how I always wanted it to be. Me and Mum and Dad, laughing together, talking together. I'd do anything to keep it that way.

It was only as I lay in bed and listened to their murmured, annoyed whispers from the living room that the old fears rose up in me again.

They were two lovely people. Why couldn't they just be happy?

*   *   *

I have never looked forward to going to school so much in my life. Dying for everyone to see and comment on my hair.

Dawn and Kaylie, waiting for me at the top of the stairs, jumped and screamed when I came into view. 'That is *so* cool!' Dawn shouted.

'I can't believe a haircut could change you like that. You look like a new person.'

It was everything I needed to hear. No one would ever mistake the other one for me now. And it wasn't just the haircut that was different. I felt it was a whole new me at school that day.

A change is as good as a holiday. I hadn't realised just how true that saying was. I was more confident, especially with everyone noticing me, and admiring my new style. It made me feel as if this was a whole new beginning for me.

Even Drew Fraser did a double take when he saw me. 'I hardly recognised you there.' Then he peered closer and grinned. 'It is the real you, isn't it? Not that other one?'

I had almost smiled at him, right up until he said that. Now I glared at him and flounced off.

Monica, I noticed, was the only one in class who

didn't remark on my hair.

Kaylie giggled as we watched her trying her best to ignore me. 'Jealousy's a terrible thing!' she whispered. And we all giggled. Was Monica really jealous of me?

But new hairstyle or not, when it came to remembering my lines for *Macbeth* at rehearsal that night, they still eluded me.

And Monica made sure I knew it.

That night we were rehearsing the scene when Macbeth first sees Banquo's ghost. Daft Donald was trying to make us believe it was every bit as scary as a *Scream* movie. I don't think. No one believed him.

Over and over in my mind I repeated my lines. 'This is the very painting of your fear; this is the air-drawn dagger . . .'

It never would come out right . . . 'the painting of your fear.' As soon as I said those words, all I could see was a portrait of myself, of my fear. Not any other ghost. My mind kept going blank.

It didn't help that Monica was sitting in the first row, right in front of me, mouthing the lines perfectly. Mocking me. I tried not to look at her.

But even then, that wonderful day didn't go wrong. When I finally got the words right, Donald came right up to me and slapped me on the back. 'You sent a shiver down my spine when you said that, Fay, gazing into the distance, almost as if you could see a ghost, too.' He rubbed his hands together with excitement. 'I knew I'd made the right choice with you.'

Poor old Monica almost fell off her seat with annoyance.

It had been a wonderful day, one of the best, and I had the whole weekend to look forward to. Shopping in the mall on Saturday with the girls. Cinema at the Multiplex at night, and best of all, and most surprising to me, was the memory of Drew Fraser's eyes, green like emeralds, following me as I walked out of rehearsal and Kaylie and Dawn's whispered words. 'I definitely think he fancies you.'

CHAPTER SIXTEEN

It was a wonderful weekend. The best weekend I'd had for ages. Even the winter sun shone bright and crisp for me.

Until Monday, which was dark and wet and miserable. Dreech, we call it here. Isn't that a good word? Sums it up perfectly. Dreech.

A drizzly rain filled the air like a mist, as I walked up the stairs to school. Kaylie and Dawn wouldn't be waiting for me at the top today. Dawn had phoned to say her mum would be running them both to school.

I held my umbrella down in front of me and hardly heard the footsteps coming behind me. Not until they stopped right beside me.

I peeked to see who the trainers belonged to and found myself looking into the green eyes of Drew Fraser. Normally, he would rush past me. Pulling at my umbrella, trying to trip me up. Acting like a dork. This morning, he had stopped and when I looked at him, he actually smiled.

'I was hoping I'd see you,' he said.

Suddenly, I was blushing. Stupid, because I'd known Drew Fraser all my life, and had never liked him. He'd never seemed to like me either. Yet, now, here we were on the stairs alone and he'd been hoping he'd see me.

Cool.

'How are you enjoying *Macbeth*?' he asked. Drew, who always seemed so sure of himself, now acted as if he didn't quite know what to say. Was that because of me? The thought made my heart race.

He didn't wait for my answer, but rushed on. 'It's a rubbish play, isn't it? I mean, it should be a good story. Murder, ghosts, witches, fighting. But the words!' He made a face as if he was going to be sick, and I laughed. 'That Shakespeare guy didn't have a clue, eh?'

He smiled at me. He really did have nice teeth. I had never noticed that before. Or how thick his lashes were. Like brushes. Then, he said something that really took me by surprise. 'Tell me about this double you've got.'

My smile disappeared. Was this what it had all been leading up to? 'Are you trying to take the mickey?'

Before I'd even finished he interrupted me. 'I'm serious, Fay. I think it's really interesting. You know anything like that always fascinated me. Anything weird and wonderful.'

I almost walked away from him then. 'Weird and wonderful! Are you referring to me?'

He slapped his hand across his mouth and laughed. 'I didn't mean that, honest.'

The way he said it made me laugh too.

'You know I've always loved things like this,' he went on, his voice full of excitement, like a little boy. 'But it's always been in books, or in movies. But this is real life, and it's happening to somebody I know.'

I didn't answer him and he went on hurriedly. 'I see you running down the stairs in front of me, sometimes you don't even look at me, as if you haven't seen me. As if I'm not there . . . and now I wonder, was that really you I saw?'

Was he being serious? He seemed to be. If so, he would be the first person who believed me. If he was, maybe I could tell him everything.

Yet, here, even on a dreech Monday morning, it all seemed to be a thing of the past. The figure in the lift, the hand on the stairwell, the lights going out in the corridor. Coincidence, accident, but nothing mysterious.

'I'm probably making too much of it,' I said, mainly because all at once I didn't want Drew to think I was potty. 'Mistaken identity. Happens all the time.'

He nodded. 'Probably.' He hesitated, wanting to say more. 'But I've been kinda looking into it, you know, on the Internet. I've found out things, strange things.' He seemed so serious then. He reached out and touched my arm. 'Things I think you should know.'

'Like what?'

He didn't get a chance to answer. There was a sudden commotion at the top of the stairs. His mates, yelling out to him. He glanced up at them and waved. Then he looked back to me and shrugged. 'Got to go,' he began backing up the stairs. 'Maybe . . .' I watched his face go red. 'Maybe I can walk down the road with you after school. Tell you about it.'

My face went as red as his. Drew Fraser was asking to walk me home. I don't even think I answered. Just swallowed and nodded. Then he was off and running up the stairs two at a time.

Wasn't it strange that only a few days ago he annoyed me so much. I couldn't stand him. Yet, in those few days it would seem my opinion of him had changed entirely. Drew Fraser asking to walk me home? And I was looking forward to it. Here was another mystery!

I was desperate to tell the girls. Forget all about the 'strange things' he wanted to talk about. Who cared about that now? Wait till Kaylie and Dawn heard this! And wouldn't moaning Monica be *so* jealous!

I almost ran up the rest of the stairs, and because it was so wet decided to sneak into school by the side door rather than walk the length of the playground to the main entrance. As soon as I was inside I shook out my umbrella and made my way as fast as I could to the girls' locker room. I hoped Kaylie and Dawn had already arrived.

Of all mornings, Daft Donald chose this one to waylay me.

'Just the girl I want to speak to,' he grinned, and beckoned me into his classroom. 'I won't keep you a minute.'

I had no choice but to step inside.

'I'm really soaking wet, sir,' I said.

'I know. I just wanted to tell you that I've asked your English teacher if he can spare you for 15 minutes during his lesson. We're going to help you get those lines right.' He grinned as if I'd be delighted.

I groaned silently. If I hadn't wanted to get the better of Monica I would have told him where to stuff his lines.

Donald nodded. 'The same expression Drew Fraser had when I told him.'

'Drew?' I asked innocently.

He smiled. 'Yes. Drew. No point Lady Macbeth learning her lines alone. Both of you are coming out of English.'

My face went bright red once again and I tried not to look too pleased. Donald only laughed. 'Mmm. Drew Fraser's face went red when I told him, too.'

This morning, I decided, was getting better by the minute.

Donald patted my shoulder. 'It's good to see you back to your old self, Fay. That haircut's done wonders for you.' I was about to agree with him when he added, 'Why I hardly recognised you when you came across the playground earlier. Not until you looked up and waved.'

A dark shadow fell across my life in that second. I shook my head. 'It wasn't me, sir. I didn't come across the playground.'

He dismissed that. 'Of course it was you. You looked up at me and waved, and I waved back.'

I drew my hands through my hair, beginning to feel breathless. Please. I didn't want all this to start again. 'That wasn't me, sir. That wasn't me!' He must have heard the panic in my voice. He took a step back and looked at me for a moment. Then he said, very softly, 'I was probably mistaken.'

But he didn't mean a word of it. He was trying to calm me down. Keep the crazy girl happy.

I stumbled out of his classroom. I'd done everything to change things, hadn't I? And still she was following me.

What was happening, and how was I going to stop it now?

As I moved towards the locker room, I could hear Monica's voice.

Well, not exactly Monica's voice. Monica's voice trying to sound like mine.

'Look at me, I'm Fay. Please notice me. I'll do anything to get attention.'

I stepped into the doorway so quietly no one saw me at first.

And what *I* saw explained everything.

There was Monica, talking like me, pretending to be me. Monica, with her hair now cut exactly like mine. And suddenly everything fell into place.

'I'll get you,' she had said that day. And she had.

It had been Monica all the time.

CHAPTER SEVENTEEN

It was all so clear to me now. Monica had sworn she'd get her revenge because I'd got the part she'd wanted. And, wasn't it then that everything had started to happen? Where had she been on the night of that first rehearsal when those footsteps had followed me down the dark corridor?

In the girls' toilets.

I could see her now, coming out of there, looking smug. Smug because I had been so afraid. She'd been in there for ages, Dawn had told me. Or had she? Had she, instead, left the auditorium and followed me, switching off the lights, one by one? Knowing she was frightening me. Then, had she darted back into the toilets before anyone noticed? Of course she had. And she could have been the girl in the flats too. She didn't live very far away from me. How easy to fool Mrs Brennan. She was blind as a bat anyway. She never saw anything beyond my shiny hair. Well, Monica had shiny hair too. Just like mine.

Now, even more like mine.

All this passed through my mind in the blink of an eye. Before anyone had even looked up and saw me standing there.

Monica saw me first. Her face went white. She at least had the decency to look guilty. I could see she was ready with a smart remark.

But I didn't give her time to say a word. I roared like a demon out of hell and ran at her. 'You! You've been doing this all along!' I caught her by the shoulders and sent her sprawling on the floor. Her friends tried to hold me back, but I had the strength of ten of them. I jumped on Monica and grabbed her hair and banged her head hard on the floor. She was too astonished to fight back. She kept screaming at me, 'You're mad! You are mad! Get her off me.'

But no one dared. They were afraid of me. Afraid of my anger.

'You're evil!' I yelled at her. 'How could you do such an evil thing!'

Now she tried to scratch me, bite me. But there was

no contest.

I had never felt such a fury. All I wanted was to make her suffer the way I had been suffering over the past few weeks.

It took two of the teachers – Mr Hardie and Mrs Williams – to drag me away from Monica. Even then I struggled to reach her. 'You don't know what she's done!' I kept shouting.

Monica struggled to her feet. She was crying, and her hair was standing on end. 'I didn't do anything. She's crazy! She's been going crazy for weeks.'

They practically carried me to Mrs Williams' office, as half the school looked on as if I was some alien creature, something to be afraid of.

Past Drew Fraser, who stared at me silently, his face puzzled. I wanted to tell him, shout out to him, 'The double was Monica all the time.' But by this time I was crying too.

Mrs Williams waited until I'd calmed down before she asked me a thing. She made tea, and made me drink it. 'I've sent for your mother and father,' she said. I began to protest but she stopped me with her hand. 'I couldn't possibly let this incident go unnoticed.' Then her voice softened. 'Fay, what is going on?'

I took a long swallow of tea and then I told her. I told her everything. Every incident, right up to today, when Donald had thought it was me in the playground. 'It was Monica,' I insisted. 'It was always Monica. You saw her, Mrs Williams. Her hair's exactly like mine. Why else would she get it cut like that unless it was to go on pretending she's me?'

'Have you never heard the saying, imitation is the sincerest form of flattery?'

'But she's not been trying to flatter me. She's been trying to frighten me. Even this morning—'

'As for this morning,' Mrs Williams interrupted. 'That certainly wasn't Monica. She came in the side door to avoid the rain. Just as you did. She has a witness to prove it.'

'Yes. One of her *friends*, I suppose,' I snapped.

'No, not one of her friends. Actually, I saw her, Fay.'

She was just saying that to shut me up. I was sure of it. I saw then that no one was ever going to believe me.

'Fay, you're turning a simple case of mistaken identity into a drama.'

'Why would I make all this up, Miss?' I asked her, near to tears.

She lifted an eyebrow. 'Perhaps you already know the

answer to that.'

I didn't understand what she meant, didn't have time to think about it, for at that moment Mum and Dad arrived together, and I could see Mum had been crying. They listened as Mrs Williams told them what had happened, listened, and couldn't quite take it in.

Mum turned to me. 'What's happening to you, Fay? All this, it just isn't like you.'

Mrs Williams simply nodded her head. 'Exactly, Mrs Delussey, and that is what I think is the crux of the matter. This just isn't like Fay.' She folded her hands together on the desk. 'There's no point pretending I don't know that there has been some difficulty at home.'

At that point Dad sat down on the other side of me. I clutched at his hand.

'Fay is a very sensitive girl. She loves both of you very much. If you two were to break up – she'd be torn in two. She wouldn't know which one to go with. So, when people have started mistaking some girl with a passing resemblance for her, she has built the whole thing up out of all proportion. She has created this other one.'

I was gaping at my teacher in disbelief. Mrs Williams was a nice woman. A good teacher. I knew she meant well. But after a two-week counselling course she was coming up with this rubbish to explain everything.

Mum turned to me. 'Can this be true, Fay?'

I could not believe my mother would be taken in by this. But there it was in her eyes, the hurt, the pain and, yes, the growing belief that this was the answer. 'I didn't realise we were hurting you this much.' She looked at Dad. 'This is our fault.'

Suddenly, I jumped to my feet. I couldn't take it anymore. 'This is rubbish! There *is* someone else pretending to be me. *Monica!* That's the simple explanation. Why can't anybody believe it?'

Mrs Williams put on her best counselling voice. 'Come on, Fay. You know there's no one pretending to be you.' She said it calmly, her voice so patronising I could have screamed.

I wouldn't listen to this anymore. The letter opener was on the desk in front of me and I grabbed it. 'Well, from now on you will definitely know when it's me!'

I dragged the sharp end right down my hand. Droplets of blood fell like rubies on to the desk. *My* blood.

Mum screamed. And I yelled, 'I'll be the one with the scar.'

CHAPTER EIGHTEEN

I was asked to stay off school for the rest of the week. Not that I could have refused. But they wouldn't suspend me. Not in my 'disturbed' condition.

And, of course, what I'd done – stabbing myself with the letter opener – only confirmed that.

Mum and Dad led me off to hospital, past my school friends in the corridor. Kaylie and Dawn looked shocked at the blood-soaked handkerchief tied round my hand. But they said nothing. And Drew Fraser just looked puzzled. Had it been only this morning that he'd suggested walking home with me? Only an hour ago that nothing else seemed to matter?

Four stitches, that was all I needed. But I spent the rest of that day in bed. I couldn't stop shivering. Mum said it was shock. But I knew what it was. It was fear. Fear that someone, if not Monica, was deliberately doing this to me, and I couldn't get anyone to believe me. I was alone. More alone than I'd ever felt in my life.

Mum came into my bedroom in the afternoon. Her eyes were red and her face puffy from crying. She was trying hard to smile now. Trying to make me feel better. All I felt was guilty.

'I'm staying off work all week,' she told me. 'I'm going to look after you. I've got some holidays from work.'

'Mum, you don't have to do that. I'll be fine on my own.' I lifted my bandaged hand. 'I won't do anything like this again.'

I couldn't imagine now, what had possessed me to do it in the first place. I must have been mad—

The phrase came into my mind, and I immediately pushed it away.

Mum stroked my face. 'Dad and I had a long talk and we've decided things are going to be different from now on. We're going to stay together. You won't ever have to worry about that again. Dad and you and me. A family. Right?'

It was all I ever wanted to hear, but it wasn't all right. Because it meant they really did believe – what Mrs Williams had said – there was no other one or anyone pretending to be me. I had made her up because I didn't want my parents to split up.

Mum hugged me. 'We're going to look for a holiday. Somewhere in the sun. After the New Year. Nice time for a winter holiday, eh?'

It was sounding better by the minute, but she still had to know I wasn't mistaken or making it up, or mad. 'Mum, someone *has* been pretending to be me.'

She nodded. 'I'm sure you're right. Girls can be really horrible at times. I remember one in my class. Rose Devenney. She used to spread the most horrible rumours about me, got all her friends to back her up. So it looked as if they were true. I couldn't get anyone to believe me either. Then, I had this most awful fight with her. In the playground. We battered lumps out of each other. But, you know, she never spread any rumours again. In fact, Rose Devenney and I became good mates. She was even at my wedding.'

She laughed at the memory.

'I can't imagine me and Monica ever being friends.'

'No. Maybe not. And I don't want you thinking I'm condoning what you did,' she scolded. 'But I think it probably was this Monica who's been playing tricks on you. But after today . . . I think it will stop. She must know she's gone too far.'

How I hoped that was true.

Mum went on. 'But it wouldn't have got to you so much if you hadn't been so worried about your dad and me.'

I wanted to tell her that was rubbish. But at that moment, I wasn't sure. I didn't know any more what was real and what was imaginary.

Her voice became so soft. 'I do love your dad, you know.'

How could she help it? My dad was wonderful, and good, and thoughtful. She could never get anyone better than him. 'Of course you do,' I said, just as softly.

That week wasn't as bad as I had expected it to be. Kaylie and Dawn came most nights, filling me in with all the news about Monica.

'She's walking about telling everybody you're off your head, but no one listens to her. Nearly everybody thinks she had it coming to her.'

'And she thought she was bound to get the part of Lady Macbeth now. She played it in rehearsal the other night and she remembered all her lines. Made a point of telling Daft Donald, and d'you know what he said?'

I was eager to know, and Dawn went on, mocking Donald's posh voice. 'This is Fay's part and it will remain Fay's part.' She laughed loudly. 'He thinks she was the one playing tricks on you as well.'

All this made me feel better. Yet, somewhere at the back of my mind a warning bell was ringing.

Monica hadn't come across the playground that day. Mrs Williams was the witness who could prove that. She'd come in the side entrance just like me.

So, who had waved at Donald?

CHAPTER NINETEEN

Mum made me apologise to Monica when I went back to school.

No. She didn't actually *make* me. She suggested I should, told me I'd feel better if I did. 'Let's look on this as a whole new beginning,' she said.

A whole new beginning was exactly what I wanted. But I was reluctant to say I was sorry to Monica. 'She doesn't deserve an apology,' I told Mum.

'Maybe she doesn't, but if you apologise and she refuses to accept it, then it puts her in the wrong.'

So, when I went back to school the following Monday, I walked straight up to Monica. She took a step back as if she thought I was about to attack her again. But I held out my hand. I even managed a smile. 'I'm sorry, Monica,' I said, there in front of the whole class. 'I'm really sorry I had that fight with you.'

Her eyes narrowed. I could see she was ready to throw one of her acid remarks at me. She didn't want to accept the apology. She glanced around, ready to tell anyone who would listen that I was crazy. But when she did she saw that every eye was on her. And she must have sensed, as I did, that she would be the one who would be crazy if she refused to accept.

She didn't smile back. That would have been expecting too much. But she did shake my hand. She didn't say anything either. Not then. Not until we were taking our seats and the classroom buzz covered her words. 'What's your game, Fay?'

But I only shrugged an answer and gave her a tiny smile.

Mrs Williams heard about my apology and took me into her office during break. 'That was a very wise thing you did.'

'It was my mum's idea,' I told her.

'But you were the one who had to actually apologise. I'm very proud of you, Fay.'

Mrs Williams was definitely beginning to annoy me. Did she really think that her being proud of me was important?

'And everything's OK at home now.' It wasn't a

question. It was a fact. Mum must have phoned and told her. I hated my teachers knowing, this one in particular. It was none of her business, and of course it only reinforced her opinion that 'family troubles' were behind my wild imaginings.

I was glad to get away from her. As I hurried down the corridor, Drew Fraser was leaning against the wall at the main doors. He was watching me come towards him, tapping a pencil against his white teeth. It didn't occur to me for a moment that he was waiting for me. But he was.

He stood straight as I came near and beckoned me across to him. 'I haven't had a chance to talk to you. Do you still want to hear what I've found out?'

I had almost forgotten. 'What have you found out?'

He glanced around almost as if he was afraid someone might be listening. 'Remember what I told you that day on the stairs?'

It seemed so long ago now. 'You said you'd found out things.' Strange things, he had told me, but I didn't mention that.

'Are you still interested?'

One thought sprang into my mind. 'Why are *you* so interested, Drew?'

He smiled. 'Because it's a mystery. And you know I've always loved mysteries.' He tugged my sleeve. 'Let's go through this whole thing. Right. You've *not* got an identical twin.'

I shook my head. 'That was the first thing I thought of.'

'And you've not been cloned.'

I sighed. 'Hardly likely, is it?'

'And Monica's not doing this.'

Now he had my complete attention. 'It has to be her.'

Drew was shaking his head. 'It's not. I've asked her. I believe her.'

I took a step away from him. 'So, you think I'm imagining everything too, do you?'

'No. And you're not potty either. I believe you, Fay. Do you know what Sherlock Holmes says?'

'Sherlock Holmes, the fictional detective. What's he got to do with this?'

'He says, once you have dismissed the probable, what you're left with, no matter how improbable, must be the truth.'

I liked the idea of that. No matter how improbable. 'So, what are you left with?' I asked.

He blew out his cheeks. 'Something so unbelievable it will blow you away.'

The bell was ringing, summoning us to our next class. 'There's something I want to show you on the Internet. Can you meet me at lunchtime? In the library?'

Dawn came rushing in through the doors just then. Stopped dead when she saw who I was talking to.

Drew began to move away. 'Lunchtime?' he asked again.

I smiled back my answer, and Dawn's eyes flashed.

'Are you meeting him at lunchtime?' She was excited at the prospect. 'Things really are looking up for you.'

I didn't tell her why he was meeting me. I wanted her to think it was because he fancied me. Yet I could hardly wait till lunchtime – 'Something so unbelievable it will blow you away.'

What could that be?

CHAPTER TWENTY

The library was always buzzing at lunchtime. Everyone went there to use the computers, whether it was to research something for homework, or more often to play games. Drew was already sitting at a computer by the window when I went in. He had drawn up a chair close to his and as I came up he looked at me and patted the chair.

I could feel lots of eyes on us, and knew what they would be thinking. That Lord and Lady Macbeth were a pair.

'Now, what's so unbelievable?' I asked. I was ready to believe anything he told me. Anything that would explain away all the strange things that had happened to me.

Drew had already logged on to a website.

Myths and Legends.

He clicked in to a page, and scrolled down the screen until he reached the information he wanted.

'Read that,' he said, and he sat back to let me move closer.

I peered at the screen.

FETCH   Irish, Celtic folklore.
A fetch (wraith) is a being who is the double of a living person. An apparition or a phantom of someone living. Since a fetch often appears as solid flesh, it is sometimes impossible to tell that it is not a real, living being. It may only be later that its true nature is revealed.
In German folklore a fetch is known as a **doppelganger.**

A fetch? I'd never heard of such a thing. 'But that's just a myth,' I said. 'You don't really think that's the answer, do you?' This was even more unbelievable than I'd expected. 'It's a legend, Drew. Like vampires and werewolves. This is real life. It can't be true.'

Drew's face was grim. 'Read on,' he said.

And I did. I read of stories from all around the world, myths and legends told around fires in far-off times. Tales of doppelgangers and wraiths and phantoms and fetches.

It was all here. An explanation for what had been happening to me. The only possible explanation, bizarre and improbable though it sounded. I had been seeing my fetch, my doppelganger all the time.

A myth as ancient as time itself, in my own town, in my own life.

'This does seem to explain everything, Drew,' I told him, and as I looked at him I realised just how serious and quiet he had become. His face seemed to have gone pale.

'There's more, Fay,' he said. 'But before you read it, are you sure you want to know? Maybe it's all finished now, and you can just forget about it.'

Maybe it was. I wanted it to be. But I had to read the rest.

'Of course I want to know. I want to know everything.'

I moved the cursor and read the words on the screen.

The fetch usually manifests itself at times when a person is in extreme danger. It is generally believed that to see one's own fetch, to come face to face with your doppelganger, is a portent of your own death. A sign that you are about to die.

CHAPTER TWENTY-ONE

We sat in complete silence for what seemed an age. 'Have you ever . . .' Drew hesitated, afraid to ask. 'Have you ever seen it yourself?'

I thought back, though my mind was in a turmoil. Saw again the hand on the staircase, the fleeting image in the lift as the doors slid closed. Did those count? I asked Drew.

'I don't think so,' he said seriously. 'From all I've read you have to come face to face. You have to see each other clearly, perhaps be close enough to touch.'

I could feel icy sweat trickling down my back. I remembered the night in the school corridor when some deep, ancient instinct had told me I mustn't let it touch me. And, suddenly, in that bright, sunlit library with pupils chatting and laughing, and computers whirring, I was afraid.

'I think this is the answer, Drew.'

He shrugged. 'I don't know, Fay. Surely things like this don't happen in real life.'

'Legends have to start somewhere, I suppose. In someone's real life.' I looked at him. 'But what started it? Why me?'

He pulled his chair closer. 'It's our age, I think. Things begin to happen at our age when we're going through so many changes ourselves. They say you can be more psychic, more open to seeing ghosts, and other supernatural phenomena. Our bodies are changing, and so are our minds.'

'But why *me*?' Everyone else was changing, too, surely? Kaylie and Dawn and Monica, and even Drew.

Drew didn't know the answer to that one. But he tried to explain it anyway. 'Some people are more open than others, I suppose.'

'So, it has nothing to do with my parents, my mum . . .' I let the words drift away. He knew what I meant. His mum had been my mum's confidante during all her problems.

'I did read that traumatic events can trigger it.'

'Mrs Williams will be pleased to hear that.' I was trying hard not to cry.

'I also wondered if the play had something to do with it,' Drew said thoughtfully. 'Donald said it had a history of bad luck, of weird things happening whenever it was put on.'

'The "Scottish Play",' I murmured. 'Maybe I'm going mad, just like Lady Macbeth.'

Drew touched my arm, then pulled it away quickly, glancing around the library to make sure no one had seen him. 'Don't think that, Fay. At least you know now that this is really happening. You're not making it up.'

I smiled at him. I wanted to tell him how much that meant to me. Someone believed me at last. But all I could say was, 'I don't want to die, Drew.'

His voice became soft. 'You're not going to die. I'll keep looking on the Internet. In books. We'll both find out as much as we can. There's got to be something we can do.' Suddenly, he grinned. 'I mean, who makes up the rules anyway? We'll change them. We'll make up new rules.'

Already he was making me feel better. I really wanted to ask him why it mattered to him what was happening to me. But I didn't dare.

'And you know now you're not on your own. I'm here. I understand.'

Who would have thought it? Drew Fraser, the boy who had tormented me so much over the years, was the only one who understood. He couldn't know, and I couldn't explain just how much that meant to me.

It was time to get back to class. I lifted my bag and stood up. All at once, a horrifying, terrifying, thought hit me. I threw myself back on the chair. 'How will you know when it's the real me?'

What if Drew were to meet the other one, and couldn't tell the difference?

'That's a good point,' he said. He thought about it briefly, then he smiled. 'We've got to have a code.'

'A code?' I repeated. 'What kind of code?'

'Whenever we meet, I'll say something to you, and you'll always answer the same way. Surely, your . . .' He hadn't wanted to say the word, but he did. 'Your fetch won't know. It'll be our secret.'

I thought it was an excellent idea. 'But what will our code be?'

'Something from *Macbeth*,' he said at once.

I groaned. 'I can never remember any lines.'

''Course you can. You can remember your favourite lines.' He smiled with the assurance that only a good-looking, popular boy can have. 'Whenever I see you I'll say my favourite line and then you'll answer with yours. They're not connected, so no one but you can give the answer.'

'I thought you said *Macbeth* was rubbish. The words were rubbish. So how come you've got a favourite line?'

He shrugged. 'Some of them aren't too bad.'

'So what is your favourite line?'

He didn't hesitate. '"Life's but a walking shadow, a poor player that struts and frets his hour upon the stage, and then is heard no more."'

Drew stopped abruptly. 'What's wrong, Fay? You're as white as a sheet.'

'It's those lines,' I said. 'They're scary. "A walking shadow." She's my *walking shadow*, Drew.' I swallowed a lump in my throat. 'And I don't want to be "heard no more".'

Drew shook his head. 'Sorry. I'll pick something else,' he said at once.

But I wouldn't let him. 'No. Those lines are so appropriate to what's been happening. Keep them.'

'So, what will you say back to me?'

My answer was easy. The only words I never did forget: '"Here's the smell of blood still. All the perfumes of Arabia shall not sweeten this little hand."'

125

CHAPTER TWENTY-TWO

It was great having a friend, someone who really believed me. Yet, it seemed in those next few days that it didn't matter whether anyone believed me or not. Nothing happened. Maybe, I kept hoping, it *was* all over.

Every morning on the stairs to school Drew would meet me and say: '"Life's but a walking shadow, a poor player that struts and frets his hour upon the stage, and then is heard no more."'

And though the words always filled me with some kind of dread, I would smile and reply: '"Here's the smell of blood still. All the perfumes of Arabia shall not sweeten this little hand."'

Then he'd draw his hand across his brow in mock relief. 'Wow! For a minute there I thought you were the doppelganger.'

Always the same thing, but I laughed every time. Then, he would rush up the stairs to join his mates. He never waited and walked up with me instead.

Not yet.

Kaylie and Dawn began to get really excited.

'I think there's a wee romance going on here,' Dawn would insist.

But there wasn't, I assured them.

Not yet.

At home, things seemed so much better too. Mum and Dad were spending time together and there were no dark looks or angry sighs. The gloom had disappeared.

From home at least. As we moved into an icy December, gloom descended on the town instead.

'I'll be glad to get away to the sun,' Mum said one morning a couple of weeks later. She was almost ready to leave for work, but was looking out on a dreech misty morning.

'We're above the clouds here, Mum,' I told her. 'Probably when you get down to ground level the sun will be shining.'

She laughed. 'Is it not supposed to be the opposite way about?'

I followed her to the door. 'Anyway, when are we going on this holiday?'

'Your dad's going to the travel agent today. Trying to book for just after the New Year. Majorca. Fancy that?'

Majorca! I thought. And the sun and the sea and a brand New Year, and Drew Fraser. Life, I decided, was getting better and better.

All I had to dread was the Christmas production of *Macbeth*.

'Why did Donald have to pick such a hard play? Nobody could remember those lines,' I moaned for the umpteenth time.

Another rehearsal. Another disaster. I hadn't a clue why Donald had had such faith in me. Although, by December even he was beginning to get worried.

Monica looked as smug as ever. 'He *has* made it as easy as possible for you,' she sneered. 'Nobody else is having a problem with *their* lines.'

If she'd been a nicer person, if I had liked her the tiniest bit, I would have insisted that Donald give her the part and let *me* be the understudy. But I couldn't stand Monica, and I would never give her that satisfaction.

Dawn and Kaylie would never let me anyway.

Whenever I hesitated over the lines they would shout them up at me, much to Donald's amusement. 'But you can't do that on the night, girls,' he would remind them.

Pity, I thought.

Drew was great too. 'It's not the end of the world if you forget them,' he kept telling me. 'Just shout at me, "You wimp, Macbeth. Have I got to do everything myself!" That's what my mum shouts at my dad.'

The one place I never met Drew, never expected to meet him, was in the lift. He lived on the second floor and never used it. If he had it wouldn't be the odd lift he would use, would it? It would be the even one.

So I was really surprised, no, more than surprised, delighted when one morning I stepped into the lift, and there he was.

'What are you doing here?' I asked him.

He actually blushed, though he still tried to look cool. 'I thought I'd take the lift for a change and it brought me up instead of taking me down.'

I didn't say anything. But that had to be a lie. Why had he got into the odd lift, unless . . . he wanted to see *me*? Could that really be the case?

'Oh, I nearly forgot,' he said suddenly. '"Life's but a

walking shadow, a poor player that struts and frets his hour upon the stage, and then is heard no more."'

I glanced at my reflection in the stainless steel. I was blushing, too, and smiling.

I decided to have some fun with him. 'Sorry?' I said.

His smile vanished. He repeated it. '"Life's but a walking shadow, a poor player that struts and frets his hour upon the stage, and then is heard no more."'

I still stared at him blankly. 'What are you on about?'

His face was going pale. He swallowed. 'Oh, blinkin' hell!'

I could see little beads of sweat forming on his upper lip.

I laughed. 'Oh, I see. That's from the play, isn't it?' I paused, pretended I was thinking hard, patting my lips with my fingers. 'Am I supposed to remember the next line?'

Drew looked at me as if he were seeing a ghost. He took a step back from me.

I moved towards him. I smiled. Glancing at my reflection even I could see the smile made my face look weird. It almost scared me. 'What's the matter, Drew?' I said in my most wicked voice.

Drew looked up at the numbers above the door. I

followed his gaze. 5-3-. It wasn't moving fast enough for him. 'Let me out of here,' he said.

It would have been too cruel to keep it up. I began to laugh, I couldn't stop laughing.

He looked puzzled. Afraid almost. Was this a mad-woman? Crazy, like Lady Macbeth?

I couldn't do it to him any longer. The lift reached the ground and I held out my hand to him. '"Here's the smell of blood still. All the perfumes of Arabia shall not sweeten this little hand."'

I have never seen anyone look so relieved in all my life. The colour flooded back into his cheeks. He fell back against the wall of the lift. 'You are horrible, Fay Delussey.' He was breathing hard. 'I was dead scared there. I cannot believe you did that to me.'

I was giggling now. 'I know, but I just couldn't resist it.'

By the time the doors opened we fell out of the lift still laughing.

And that morning Drew walked with me the whole length of the stairs, and didn't run on until we reached Dawn and Kaylie, waiting for me with big grins on their faces.

CHAPTER TWENTY-THREE

Drew and I spent almost every lunchtime in the school library now, at the computer, finding out as much as we could about fetches and doppelgangers.

Everything we discovered only made me more afraid.

Stories and legends of strange meetings. Dead soldiers coming back from the war for one last moment with a loved one. Sitting, solid and real, in a fireside chair. The living, breathing image of the soldier who, at that same instant, was dying on a faraway battleground.

The strange story of a woman, lying in bed and opening her eyes to see her husband standing by the window looking out across the fields. Half asleep, she turned and there he was, that same husband, flesh and blood and bone, lying in the bed beside her. Which was the real one? She couldn't tell. All she knew was that within a month, her husband was dead and buried.

The chilling tale of the villagers who stoned a woman to death, convinced she was the fetch and not the real person, and that what they had done was no sin, no crime, because a fetch had no soul.

Yet, however much we read, or what we found out, it always came back to the same thing. No matter what culture the legend came from, no matter in what time the myth emerged, to see your own image was a portent of your own death.

A portent.

The word haunted me.

'I don't want to die, Drew,' I would say. 'I'd much rather find out that it was Monica pretending to be me.'

'You're not going to die, Fay,' he would always insist. 'I told you, we're going to change the rules.'

But how were we going to change the rules, I wanted to ask him. How could I, when he didn't know the answer to that either. However, just knowing he was there, that he understood, always made me feel better.

'Anyway, maybe I don't have to worry about it anymore. It's been over two weeks now, and nothing's happened.'

He grinned. 'Maybe it's finished,' he said.

That thought cheered me. Finished. I so wanted it to

be. But somewhere deep inside the thought remained: why had it started in the first place? Why me?

Of course, I might have suspected, Mrs Williams had the answer.

'Everything fine now, dear?' She stepped out of her office one day as I was passing. The way a spider leaps at a fly.

'Everything's fine.' I knew Mum phoned her – kept her informed about how I was doing at home. I'd been annoyed about that. Didn't like teachers knowing our business, especially an amateur psychiatrist like Mrs Williams.

She touched my arm reassuringly. As if I needed reassurance from her. 'Yes, dear. I knew it would all sort itself out when things at home were more settled.'

I wanted to yell at her. I hadn't imagined anything, or made anything up. There really had been another one of me. But I knew she would never listen. In her mind, her solution had worked.

And maybe it had. Things were getting better all round for me. And that other, my fetch, my doppelganger, it seemed, had disappeared.

Then, it happened.

One day after school I walked straight into town by myself. I was looking for Christmas presents for Kaylie and Dawn. Dreaming of maybe getting one from Drew Fraser.

It was as I was coming out of the Forum where the small market stalls were that I saw them.

Mum, and him.

The man she'd been seeing before. I'd only ever caught a glimpse of him once, in a car with her, but I'd never forget his face. How could she prefer him to Dad? He wasn't half as good looking. I stepped into a doorway to watch them. They were standing on the pavement as if they'd just met accidentally. Old friends sharing a moment together. They looked innocent. No one watching them would imagine there was anything guilty about that meeting. Except me.

To me, they looked uncomfortable, as if they didn't know what to say to each other. As if they didn't know how to make small talk.

They were smiling at each other, but neither of them looked happy. As I watched, I felt as if my heart had stopped beating. As if I was caught in time.

Then, they said goodbye. Mum turned away, and I saw her face. The smile disappeared. She blinked, bit her lip, trying hard not to cry. Even I could see that. I watched her as she ran towards the taxi rank, wanting to be away from him quickly so he wouldn't witness her tears.

I watched him too. He ran on across the street. Then he turned and his eyes searched her out, found her and never left her till the taxi she was in moved out of sight. There was pain in his face. And love.

He loved her.

He loved my mum.

And she still loved him. I was sure of it. She still loved him. Though she'd given him up and stayed with me and Dad, and promised never to leave. She still loved *him*.

She'd given him up for me. Forever. Because some daft teacher had made her believe that I was having delusions because of her affair, because I couldn't face her leaving.

That was rubbish.

I forgot the presents. I slowly walked the long road home, as the darkness closed around me, and the icy mist descended on the town. I couldn't bear the thought of my mum being unhappy. Yet I couldn't bear the thought of losing her.

Christmas presents were forgotten. Everything else was forgotten.

What was going to happen now?

CHAPTER TWENTY-FOUR

She was home by the time I got back. Standing in the kitchen, preparing chicken for tea. She turned to face me as I walked in, and smiled. 'Good day at school?'

I searched her face for any signs of guilt, or sadness. But there was nothing. She chatted away while she made the tea, and when Dad came in with the holiday brochures they both pored over them.

Had I been mistaken? Maybe she didn't care about him at all. Or was she just putting on a brave face?

'I'd rather you didn't use that odd lift, Fay,' Dad said as we sat at the table. 'There was somebody else stuck in it today. For two hours.' He looked at Mum. 'What's been happening with that petition you got up?'

'If we don't hear anything by next week,' Mum said, 'we're sending a committee to the Council offices. We have to do something. It's a death trap that thing.'

And so, they chatted on, about the holiday, and Christmas and the odd lift. And not a sign of the pain I had seen earlier that day on my mum's face.

I wished I could understand. Maybe when you were older things fell into place. But for now, I was just confused.

It was all I could think about all night, and in my dreams Mum and Dad and this other man were all stuck in the lift, not talking to each other. I was there, too, but they couldn't see me. I was trapped behind the mirrored steel. And that was the most frightening thing of all.

Mum and Dad had both left for work by the time I was ready for school. Mrs Brennan was already waiting at the lift. Pension day.

'Hello, darlin',' she said, beaming at me. 'You look that bonny with your hair like that, do you know?'

I hardly listened, my mind was still a jumble of confused thoughts. The lift came and the doors slid open. 'It's actually working today,' Mrs Brennan said. 'It's a miracle.'

I took one step into the lift and drew back. 'Could you send it back up for me, please, Mrs Brennan? I've forgotten something.'

'I'll hold it for you if you like. I'm not in a hurry. That wee Gupta's always sleeping in. The post office won't be opened yet.'

I shook my head. 'No, Mrs Brennan. Thanks all the same.'

I didn't want her to wait for me, because I had come to a decision. I wasn't going to school today. I couldn't face talking to people, and listening and trying to learn. When all I wanted to do was to be alone, and think.

All I needed, I thought, was one day completely to myself to think things through.

There was a thrill in being in the flat by myself. Being able to watch television if I wanted, to have the place filled with noise, or silence. My choice.

I made some coffee and settled myself in the chair by the window. The mist hung low over the hills and seeped through around the town. Would Drew miss me, I wondered? Then I remembered that Drew wasn't going to school today either. He had a five-a-side tournament to attend.

Would Kaylie and Dawn think I'd gone with him? That we'd stayed off school together? How cool would that be?

I had caused Mum and Dad so much worry over the past few weeks. I didn't want them to worry about me again. I loved them both so much.

But, if they ever split up, I'd love them both the same. I'd handle it. Other people did.

The phone rang, but I ignored it. Kaylie or Dawn probably wanting to know where I was. Let them wonder. I'd tell them tomorrow.

It was a good decision staying off school that day. It was exactly what I needed to prepare myself for whatever might happen in the future. I felt happy that day. Together or separate, I wanted Mum and Dad both to be happy too.

By the time they came in from work, I was poring over homework. 'Good day?' Mum asked, hanging her coat in the hall cupboard.

'Brilliant!' I answered. And I hadn't lied. It had been a good day. Lots of decisions reached and a whole new future ahead.

CHAPTER TWENTY-FIVE

Next morning, Mum and I met Mrs Brennan at the lift. 'Did you get it OK yesterday, dear? I sent it back up for you.'

Was I glad I'd seen Mrs Brennan yesterday? Proof to Mum if she'd been suspicious that I had gone to school like a good little girl.

'Yes, Mrs Brennan. Got it fine.'

'We're taking our lives in our hands using it,' Mrs Brennan said cheerily. As if plunging to our deaths down the lift shaft had a funny side.

Mum laughed too. 'Yes, don't tell your dad. He's warned us to use the stairs, at least to the next floor so we can catch the even lift.'

When Mum kissed me goodbye she looked at me thoughtfully. 'There's something different about you today. What is it?'

I knew exactly what it was. I felt different. But I only smiled at her and began to hurry towards the steps. 'It's Christmas!' I shouted excitedly, throwing my bag in the air.

Drew Fraser was dawdling ahead of me. I was so full of confidence I called out to him to wait. We quickly checked our code lines, then I asked, 'How did your five-a-sides go?'

He grinned. 'Foregone conclusion.' He poked at his chest. 'This boy's brilliant.'

'And so modest.' I laughed.

'We've got the final rehearsal for *Macbeth* tomorrow,' he said.

I groaned. 'Don't remind me. I'm going to be rubbish.'

He only shrugged. 'Who cares? It'll be a laugh.'

He began picking the weeds off the wall and he muttered something.

'Sorry?' I asked. 'I didn't hear that.'

He glanced at me shyly. His ears went red and he licked his lips. 'I said . . . want to go with me to the Christmas disco at school?'

If I'd been happy before I was ecstatic now. Drew Fraser, asking *me* to go with him to the Christmas disco!

I held out my hand to him, grinning. 'All the perfumes of Arabia . . .' I began, 'wouldn't stop me.'

He looked as pleased as I felt. 'Brilliant.'

His friends called to him from the top of the stairs but I couldn't make them out in the mist. 'Better go,' he said. 'Don't want to bump into your giggling pals.'

But Kaylie and Dawn weren't waiting for me at the top of the stairs this morning. I didn't see them till I hurried into the playground just as the bell was ringing. We filed into the class together. I was dying to tell them about Drew, but I wanted to pick exactly the right moment. Preferably when Monica was within earshot.

It was Mr Hardie's class first and as we took our seats I remembered with dismay that he had timetabled a test for us yesterday. And I had missed it. I prayed he wouldn't ask me to stay behind today to do it.

I leaned across to ask Kaylie how hard it had been but I didn't get the chance. Mr Hardie slammed a jotter down on his desk to shut us all up.

'Well,' he began. 'I have to say you all surprised me yesterday.'

Everyone looked bewildered.

'I certainly knew that some of you were thick.' Suddenly his voice roared. 'I just didn't realise the whole blinking lot of you were.'

Everyone glanced about sheepishly. Mr Hardie started striding about looking from one of us to the other. His eye finally fell on me and his eyebrow rose.

'Except, to my amazement . . . young Fay here.'

I looked around at everyone and smiled. He would soon find out I was thick, too, when I actually did the test. He stepped towards me and slapped a jotter on the desk in front of me. 'You got top marks. Hardly a question wrong. How did you manage it?'

My mouth went dry. He was winding me up. 'Pardon, sir?'

He nodded. 'Surprised you as well, didn't it?' He opened the jotter and pointed. 'There you go. Top marks. Congratulations.'

I went ice cold at what I saw.

My name.

My handwriting.

And the date.

Yesterday.

CHAPTER TWENTY-SIX

'Is something wrong, Fay?' Mr Hardie bent down to me. I must have gone so pale, like a ghost. I could feel sweat form on my top lip. I was shaking my head. I pushed the jotter away from me as if it was contaminated.

'This isn't mine, sir,' I said. My voice sounded strange – disembodied, as if it didn't belong to me.

Mr Hardie found that funny. 'Exactly what I thought, Fay. Even when you were sitting there doing the test, I kept watching you and thinking, I've never seen our Fay looking so intent during a science test. But, there you are, you proved me wrong.'

Unsteadily, I got to my feet. I had to make him understand. 'No, sir. I don't know who did that test, but it wasn't me. I wasn't at school yesterday.'

I heard both Kaylie and Dawn gasp. I looked across

at them. 'I wasn't. Honest.'

Kaylie's eyes went wide. 'You liar, Fay. We had a great day yesterday. A terrific laugh. Don't you remember?'

'It wasn't me!'

Why wouldn't they believe me? But they didn't. I could see it in their faces. Those looks were plainly saying, 'Here she goes again.'

They had to believe me. I was so frightened by now I was shivering. 'It was that other one. Don't you see? I stayed at home. I was there all day.'

Mr Hardie turned away in annoyance. 'This is nonsense!'

I stepped after him, pulled at his sleeve to make him face me. 'Somebody was here, pretending to be me!'

His face looked like thunder now. 'You're trying to tell me that the girl who walked in that door yesterday, and smiled at me, who sat at that desk and produced a neat, efficient piece of work, wasn't you?'

I was nodding wildly.

The teacher was sure he was being made a fool of. He exploded. 'Well, let me tell you, I hope she pretends to be you more often, because she's smarter, brighter and far more rational than you are today.'

He took my breath away. He preferred the other one. The one who was stealing my life. I looked around the class. At my friends, at Monica, at Drew. Did they all feel like that?

Monica certainly did. 'Well said, sir!' she shouted. He told her to keep quiet but she still looked smug. Kaylie and Dawn surely must have seen a difference? But already I could see the annoyance in Dawn's face. 'I thought you were back to your old self yesterday,' she said.

That's when I hit the roof. 'Back to my old self! This *is* my old self. That other one isn't me!'

I grabbed at her blazer. I didn't want to hurt her. I'd never hurt Dawn. I just wanted to make her believe me.

But after the incident with Monica, no one was taking any chances. Suddenly, two of the other girls were holding me back. 'I wasn't at school yesterday. I stayed at home!' I yelled.

Mr Hardie drew in his breath. 'Get her to Mrs Williams.'

I struggled wildly. Mrs Williams, my least favourite teacher. 'She won't listen to me,' I shouted. 'I'll prove I wasn't at school!' I shouted as I was bundled out of the classroom. But even as I said it I knew I couldn't. Mum and Dad had both been at work all day and when they'd come in, hadn't I told them what a great day I'd had? Implying that great day had been at school. The only one who had seen me yesterday had been Mrs Brennan, as I had waited at the lift in my school uniform. And she had sent the lift back up for me. I had confirmed that today, to Mum.

No one could prove I hadn't come to school.

Not even Drew.

He hadn't been at school either. If only he had he would have used the code and he at least would have known the truth.

Mrs Williams was all concern. She really did feel, she told me, inclining her head to one side like a demented bird, that I needed professional help.

'You think I'm crazy!' I yelled at her.

'Not at all, Fay. You just need help to get over this trauma.'

She wanted to phone my mother at work, but I wouldn't let her. What could she say? I calmed down as I sipped tea and she suggested I might like to go home.

I almost did – but an awful thought struck me. What if the other one came in as I left and took my place again?

I couldn't bear it.

Because that was the scariest thing. For the first time, this other one had spoken, she had been with my friends, taken my place. And no one had noticed the difference.

And if I were to come face to face with her . . . would that be the end of me?

Mrs Williams left me in her office to rest. I leaned back in the chair and closed my eyes. I rocked myself back and forth, but I didn't sleep. Once I heard the door open quietly and sensed someone watching me. I was too terrified to look, because what if it wasn't Mrs Williams?

What if it was the other one, looking in at the door, watching me and smiling? Waiting for her chance to take over . . . for good.

CHAPTER TWENTY-SEVEN

In the end I *had* to go home. I couldn't stop shaking and I could see that Mrs Williams was full of genuine concern about me. Maybe she wasn't such a bad old bird after all.

'You promise you'll tell your mother about this,' she insisted.

I assured her I would, over and over again. I didn't want any of her phone calls to my mother asking awkward questions. Asking if anything had changed in the family to make me behave like this again.

Because that bothered me too. Something had changed, hadn't it? I'd seen my mum with *that man* and suddenly, the other one had come back.

Was that the reason?

No! I couldn't, wouldn't believe that. Yet, what was the alternative? A horror I just couldn't face.

A portent of my own death.

I was going to die.

She was so close now, this other one, almost in my shoes. Maybe that meant my death was close too.

Near lunchtime, Mrs Williams asked Kaylie and Dawn to take me home. I was glad of the chance to talk to them. Perhaps I could convince them of the truth.

Some hope.

'Who are you trying to kid, Fay?' I could see Dawn was still annoyed with me. 'We were with you the whole day. We met you at the top of the stairs. We had our lunch together in the canteen.'

Kaylie, concerned as she was, was equally adamant I was lying. 'You had burger and chips. Remember?'

'Of course I don't remember. It wasn't me.'

But how could I expect them to believe such an incredible notion?

Dawn was still looking for rational explanations. 'Maybe that's it. You don't remember. You've got amnesia. Or a split personality.'

I stopped on the misty stairs and stamped my feet. 'Don't you understand, I can remember everything about yesterday. I was at home all day. Right?'

Dawn shrugged her shoulders. 'You've got nobody to prove that, have you?'

And she was right. There was nobody.

'You're my best friends,' I said as we reached my flats. 'I thought I could rely on you to believe me. Even Mr Hardie noticed I was different yesterday.'

Kaylie let out a long-suffering sigh. 'Yes. We are your best friends. So why are you trying to make fools of us?'

Dawn agreed with her, as if they'd discussed it and wanted to have it out with me. 'You can tell the truth now. It was a great joke. But it *was you yesterday*. Admit it.'

'Believe what you like!' I snapped and I pushed the button for the lift. 'Some friends you are!'

It was all the excuse they needed to turn angry and walk away from me.

'I'm not coming back to school today, by the way!' I shouted after them. 'So if you think it's me, it won't be!'

They didn't even answer me. I wondered if they would ever talk to me again.

It was only as I stepped into the lift, alone, that I realised just how frightened I really was.

Because, *she* was staring at me. In the mirror. My reflection. Or was it really the other one, ready to step through the glass and take over my life? I didn't take my eyes off her as the lift rose creakily to the 13th floor. I watched, terrified, waiting for a movement that wasn't mine. A lift of the eyebrow, a wicked smile. But the face that stared back at me was as pale and terrified as my own.

The flat was eerily quiet too. This time I didn't savour the solitude or the silence. I switched on the television even though it was just some stupid chat show, and the radio, too, so I could hear music, people talking.

Normal, wonderful, everyday life.

Then I sat on the sofa and cried.

I cried because I didn't understand what was happening. I cried because I was afraid of how all this was going to end.

I fell into a fitful sleep, until the phone ringing woke me with a start. I let it ring for a moment or two. If it was Mum, how would I explain my presence at home? But then, why would Mum phone knowing I was at school? I grabbed the receiver just before it clicked into the answering service. 'Hello?'

There was someone there. Even though I couldn't hear breathing, or backgound noise, I knew there was someone on the other end of that line.

You always do, don't you?

Someone who wasn't answering.

I was sure suddenly that I knew who that someone was.

'Speak to me!' I yelled. 'Why are you doing this to me? Who are you?'

I was answered by silence.

'Stop it!' I screamed. 'Stop it, or else!'

I was crying now, and was about to slam down the phone in anger when, very softly, a voice answered me.

'Or else . . . what?'

And the voice was mine.

CHAPTER TWENTY-EIGHT

Too scared to scream. I threw the phone from me and found I couldn't make a sound.

The voice was mine.

Calling me, at the other end of the line.

I backed away, my eyes never leaving the receiver as it dangled against the floor. Watching it, as if I almost expected her – Who? . . . Me? – to ooze from the very phone itself.

I couldn't stay in the flat alone. I needed company, normality, people. I ran, hauled open the front door and ran, not caring whether or not it banged shut behind me.

Where was I going? I couldn't think straight.

The voice was mine. That was all I could think.

I pressed for the lift. Watched it rising floor by floor. Would have stepped into it, but suddenly knew I couldn't take the chance. The other one might be there, waiting for me, and I'd be outnumbered, because my reflection would be in there too.

If I had to come face to face with my . . . fetch, it would be on my terms.

School would almost be ready to come out. Drew. He would be coming home by the stairs. If I could see Drew and talk to him, I'd feel better. He'd know what to do.

I clattered down the stairs, flight after flight, taking the steps two at a time. My mind in a breathless turmoil.

The other one had been at school yesterday, instead of me, and now this. My voice on the phone, threatening me.

Moving ever closer.

A portent.

No!

When I reached the bottom and ran into the street the fog was closing in, growing thicker with the dusk. People moved in and out of it, emerging and then being swallowed up and disappearing. I looked all around, sure I would see *her*, stepping out, beckoning to me.

'Whoa! Hold on there!'

I gasped as I almost collided with my mother. She grabbed me by the shoulders. 'Where are you going now?'

I so wanted to tell her, hesitated, trying to find the right words. How do you explain something as strange as this?

'You're so pale, Fay.' She stroked my face. 'No wonder they sent you home from school.'

So, Mrs Williams *had* phoned her, after saying she wouldn't! Trust a teacher.

'They told you,' I muttered, the first words I'd managed since the phone call.

Mum smiled. 'No, silly, *you* told me. Remember?'

Icy sweat trickled down my spine. My heart thumped. '*I* told you?'

Mum just carried on. 'It was so nice being together this afternoon, Fay. Just you and me. I'm so glad you came down to the office to meet me. It gave us a chance to talk. Get a lot of things sorted out.'

I felt as if the wind had been punched out of me. *She* had known I would be alone, and she'd taken my place again. But this was the worst. Worse than the phone call, and the voice – my voice.

The *other one* had been with my mum. And Mum hadn't known the difference.

I wanted to tell her, shout at her, 'That wasn't *me*!' But my voice wouldn't come.

My own mother hadn't known the difference.

'What's wrong, Fay?' Her eyes were full of concern. 'Come on, we'll go home and I'll make us a nice cup of tea. Forget about talking to Drew. I knew you would never find him on the stairs anyway.' She glanced across at the stairs, barely discernible in the thick fog. 'I told you, you wouldn't find anyone in this fog.'

I followed her gaze. The other one would be there, on the stairs, waiting for Drew. I pulled away from Mum and began to run.

'Fay! Fay, are you all right?'

I glanced back at my mother. She was watching me with puzzled eyes. Then, like someone in a dream she was swallowed up by the fog.

I had only one thought in my head. I turned and ran. Ran for the stairs.

I ran after the other one.

CHAPTER TWENTY-NINE

This was it. She was too close. Taking over my whole life.

Talking to my mother. And my mother hadn't known it wasn't really me.

No!

I wouldn't take this any longer. Not for one more day.

She'd left my mother and headed for the stairs, minutes ago. Seconds ago.

She'd still be here.

This time she wouldn't get away. This time I would see her. Come face to face with her.

A portent of my own death. Could I face that?

No! I wouldn't let that be true. Who makes up the rules? Drew had said that.

Well, from now on I was making up new rules. My

rules. A new legend would begin today.

The fog swirled around me as if it were alive, growing thicker by the minute. Filling me with a sense of doom.

Sounds were strange in that fog. Strange and distant. A horn tooting somewhere in the town below, a dog whining in a nearby garden. The fog swirled around the overhanging lamps on the walls and between the branches of winter-dead trees. They reached out at me like ghostly fingers.

I stopped, breathless, and heard her. Feet stopping just like mine.

She was there. Somewhere on the steps above me.

'Come down here and face me, ya bitch!' I shouted, and my own voice seemed cloaked in the mist too.

It echoed. Or had she called out to me, too?

'*Nowwww!*' I yelled as loud as I could. Let the word ring out for so long it seemed to hang in the air.

And then, after an eternity, her feet began to move. Step by step, closer and closer.

This was it. Right or wrong. I was going to see her at last. Face to face.

A portent.

* * *

For an instant, just an instant, the mist cleared and I saw a faint figure moving towards me. A shape, unformed, ghostly. And I stood straight and tried not to be afraid.

And I remembered another day, just like this so long ago, when I had waited on these same stairs for a figure coming through the fog.

I remembered how I had pressed myself against this same wall, so frightened as I wondered, what would be the most terrifying thing that could come out of the fog?

And suddenly, here on a dark December afternoon I had the answer.

The most terrifying thing that could come out of the fog was . . .

Another me.

CHAPTER THIRTY

I wasn't breathing. No sound. No heartbeat. It was as if I was already dead.

NO!

The figure moved. A shape, a shadow, a wraith.

A fetch.

Like something from a nightmare she emerged from the fog and I gasped with the shock of it.

She was me! Her face, her hair, her eyes.

Me.

Yet, she couldn't be me. I was standing here. Alive.

I dug my nails into the palms of my hands and felt the pain. I am me. I kept telling myself over and over.

She moved towards me, not as if she were walking at all. As if she were floating, and I took a terrified step back.

'Who are you?' My voice came out in breathless gasps.

She smiled then, but it was a cold, wintry smile. 'I'm you, of course.'

The voice on the phone. My voice.

I clasped my hands over my ears. 'No! I'm me. There can't be two of us. It's not possible.'

'But there is,' she said. How like me she sounded. Then she added the chilling words. 'But not for long.'

'What do you mean by that?' I asked, though I wasn't certain I wanted to know the answer.

'Only one of us can go on,' she said softly. 'And it's going to be me.'

I didn't understand. 'But you're supposed to be . . .' The word haunted me but it had to be said. 'A portent of my death . . . aren't you? That's why you're here . . . isn't it?'

She took an age to answer me. 'I'm changing the rules.'

That's what I had thought, wasn't it? That I would change the rules.

She was so much me that she had had the same thought. She was going to change the rules. Create a new legend.

I knew then that she didn't mean me to die, only to be . . . replaced. Replaced by her.

'And what's going to happen to me . . .?' I said.

She lifted her shoulders in a shrug. 'You'll go where I've been all this time. You'll be the reflection in the glass. The shadow on the wall.'

The walking shadow, I thought, knowing now why those words had frightened me so much.

'Only, I won't ever let you out!' Her voice was vicious then.

And who would know, I thought? Who had known yesterday, when she'd walked in my shoes, talked to my friends; or today, when she'd talked to my mother? No one would know the difference.

'I might as well be dead,' I said.

But this would be worse than death. To be trapped in her world, for eternity?

'I want to live.' We both said it at once.

There in the fog we faced each other, and in that moment I realised that if I wanted to survive, I would have to be stronger than she was.

She took a step towards me. 'I'm not going back. I'm taking over.'

I shook my head, moving away from her. '*No.* I won't let you.'

'You're too late,' and the way she said it I was even

more afraid. If she came close enough to touch me, would she merge into me? Seep into my flesh, my bones? So that I would be gone for ever?

Closer again, and still her eyes never left mine. As if she was trying to hypnotise me. 'You won't feel a thing.'

Those words jerked me back into life. I stumbled backwards. 'NO!' I screamed, and I turned away from her and began to run.

'You can't run from me,' she called, and when I risked a glance back it seemed she was still close behind me.

I ran faster because I wanted to live. I had never wanted anything so much in all my life.

Her voice seemed ever closer no matter how quickly I ran. I had to get out of this fog, I wanted people around me. Life. Noise.

Yet, as I plunged down the stairs I could still sense her close, feel her cold breath through my hair.

Her voice at times like a whisper, the whisper of a siren, 'Come back to me.'

I shut her words out and ran on. On and on, through the fog.

It was as if the whole world had disappeared and all around there was only the fog and her and me.

In the distance, at last, I could see dim, ghostly lights.

The flats.

If I could make the flats. The lift. I would be safe. Away from her.

If only I could see someone. A neighbour. Someone from school. Anyone.

Where was everyone?

I was alone.

Alone in the world.

I ran into the flats and punched hard against the lift buttons.

'Hurry up!' I yelled, all the time watching for her, watching as the fog drifted menacingly into the entrance to the flats. Moving closer. 'Hurry up!'

The lift came at last. At the same moment she seemed to materialise out of the fog.

And the lift doors slid open.

EPILOGUE

Daft Donald couldn't stop grinning. 'Best rehearsal we've ever had! You're all going to be great!'

He came right across to me and slapped me on the back. 'Especially you, Fay. You were wonderful. I knew you would be.'

I smiled back. 'Thank you, sir.'

He walked away to congratulate Drew Fraser, and Kaylie and Dawn headed my way.

Kaylie was dancing with excitement. 'That Drew Fraser hasn't taken his eyes off you the whole day! Think there's a wee romance going on there.'

And this time I didn't contradict her. 'He's asked me to the Christmas disco,' I told them smugly.

Their eyes went wide at the same time. 'Ya dancer!' Dawn screamed. 'I knew he liked you. And I knew you liked him too. In spite of all you used to say about him!'

She started to mimic me. Rabbiting on about Drew. '"He's such a weirdo! He's got skeletons and vampires hanging in his room. He loves horror stories, and ghost stories. Weirdo!"' She giggled. 'Some weirdo.'

I just smiled. 'People change. He did used to be a weirdo . . . now . . . he's cool.'

The girls loved it. Dawn was almost in a frenzy. 'Poor old Monica is going to be as green as the snot in her nose.'

We all looked across at Monica. Her face was grim and she was looking at us too. Wondering what we were finding so amusing. Wondering, correctly, if it was her.

I laughed too. 'Isn't she just?'

'Yeah, especially when she was sure you had to have been in that lift when it fell last night.' Kaylie grabbed at my arm. 'Oh, Fay, we were so sure you had to be in it. We heard the fire brigades and the news spread around the town like wildfire.'

Dawn gave me one of her dramatic hugs. 'It was a terrible accident. It's a miracle no one was hurt. Weren't you lucky you weren't in it, Fay?'

'Wasn't I,' I said.

Dawn pulled at Kaylie's arm. 'We just have to drop this piece of Christmas cheer in Monica's lap, right now.

I'll just say . . . "Guess what?" And you say . . . "What, Dawn?" and I'll say, "Drew's asked Fay to the Christmas disco!" She will die, so she will.' She hauled Kaylie along. 'Come on. This should be fun.'

I saw Drew watch them go and venture towards me. He'd heard us talking about the accident.

'You were so lucky last night. You must have just missed being in it. I saw you. I was coming down the stairs, and I heard voices. I couldn't see a thing in the fog, but I was sure it was your voice. And then I saw you running down the stairs and I ran after you. I shouted, but you didn't hear me. I was dying to ask you about Hardie's test. Everybody was talking about it. It was *so* weird.'

'You saw me?' I asked.

'You were running like a bat out of hell. As if you were chasing someone . . . or running away from them. I couldn't catch you.' He shook his head. 'The lift collapsed right after that. I thought, I was sure, you must have been in it.' I could actually see him shiver. 'And d'you know what I thought? A portent of your own death. It had been true after all.'

'But it's not. I'm here. I did get into the lift, but I was so scared I jumped out again before the doors closed. I

170

was scared to use it because of *her*. In case she got in with me. Best decision I ever made. So, here I am. I'm alive. Safe and sound.'

One day I would tell him all that had happened. But not now.

'But you did see her, didn't you . . . the other one?'

I said nothing, I couldn't bear to even think about it now, but something in my eyes made him take a step back, away from me. He looked at me as if he was seeing me for the first time. 'You saw her?'

Still I didn't answer him.

'You sound different today, somehow . . . more confident. I've been thinking that since you came in.' He hesitated for a second, then he recited slowly and deliberately, '"Life's but a walking shadow, a poor player that struts and frets his hour upon the stage, and then is . . ."' there was another long hesitation, '"heard no more."' He stopped, waiting for me to reply.

I sighed. I was tired of all this. 'Haven't we had enough of this play?'

'Humour me,' he said. 'Just one more time.'

I pouted like a little girl. 'For the very first time I remembered all the lines, and now you want me to remember some more.' I shrugged. 'Sorry, my mind's gone a complete blank.'

Drew had gone pale. 'Don't wind me up, Fay, please.'

My face must have looked totally puzzled.

'You really don't know what I'm talking about, do you?' He shook his head. 'I've been wondering because you did remember all the lines. You've never done that before.'

'There's a first time for everything,' I said, touching his arm. He recoiled as if I had burned his flesh.

'But now, Fay, you don't know how to answer me. That was always how I was going to know the difference. That was our code.'

'I see. A code?' I tapped my nail against my teeth. 'I love puzzles. Those were your favourite lines . . . so, logically, I'm supposed to answer with something like . . . my favourite lines?'

The longer I hesitated, the whiter Drew's face became.

I flashed him a smile. 'Like . . . "Here's the smell of blood still. All the perfumes of Arabia shall not sweeten this little hand."'

He almost collapsed with relief. He began to laugh. The colour flooded back into his face. 'You are something else, Fay. You really are!'

I laughed too. 'I can't believe you fell for that.'

'I know. Again.'

'Again?' I asked, but he wasn't listening.

'I was pure scared there. I was sure, for just a minute, that you were that other one. That maybe I had seen her chasing you last night, and that she'd caught you. She'd taken you over. That maybe she was the one who had changed the rules. She didn't want you to die at all. When she spent the day as you, taking Hardie's test, she realised she liked life. She just wanted your life.' Relief was written all over his face. 'I'm so glad I was wrong.'

I wanted to tell him part of it anyway. 'I did come face to face with her, Drew. And yet, I'm the one who's alive.'

'Do you know what I think, Fay . . . I think she *was* a portent of your death, coming closer all the time. I think, you were meant to die in that lift . . . End of story. A portent of your own death. And yet, in a strange way, she actually saved your life. Because of her, you were too afraid to take the lift. You took the stairs instead. The lift crashed, and you lived. It actually makes my blood run cold to think about it.'

I hadn't thought of it that way, but perhaps he was right.

'But do you know what really scared me, Fay?' He looked so serious.

'What?' I asked him.

'I realised that if you were the other one, how could I really prove you weren't the real Fay?'

I smiled. 'The code, of course. Hadn't we worked out a code?'

'But if the other one had taken over as you ... wouldn't she know your favourite lines? Maybe she'd even know mine.'

'Don't say that, Drew. Does that mean, you're still not sure?'

He studied me carefully, thinking that over.

I grinned. 'Drew, it's finished. Trust me.' This time when I touched his arm, he didn't move. In fact, he drew just a fraction closer. 'I don't think I'm going to have any more problems. I'm the one who is alive. Trust me.'

The Christmas disco was before me, and a holiday in Majorca. And Mum and Dad together. Forever.

And life. Life now lay before me as well. Wonderful, exciting life. I threw back my head and I laughed loudly.

Because *she* was the other one, and I was going to make sure it stayed that way.